Cream

Christiana Harrell

Photo Credit: (c) B. Austin / www.fotosearch.com

Edited By: Trelani M. Duncan

Email the author: wordsRmylife86@yahoo.com

First Edition

Visit: Christiana-harrell.com

ISBN-13: 978-1491096147

ISBN-10: 1491096144

"It's easy to take off your clothes and have sex. People do it all the time. But opening up your soul to someone, letting them into your spirit, thoughts, fears, future, hopes, dreams... that is being completely naked."

Rob Bell

Books by Christiana Harrell

Girl-A Story for Every Les Being
Girl-Six Color Society
The D in Drama
The Replacement Man
Impossible Standards
Among Us
Beneath the Surface
Intermission

One

Junction City, Kansas

Only broke people say money isn't everything. I'd never let that lie cross my lips. I needed money, needed it in the worse way, and there were no limits on what I'd do to get it. I didn't grow up with much, living from foster home to foster home, calling no woman mother and no man father. I couldn't even believe in God because I had never been introduced to him.

I had very few possessions to my name. A name that I only knew because of what someone told me. I owned one oversized no-name-brand duffle bag that I selected from a box of donations when I was twelve. I felt safer with my few belongings inside of something and it was the only reason I took it. It had a little rip on the side, but I didn't care because anything handed down was expected to have a cosmetic issue. I was just excited that the zipper worked and it belonged to me. I filled it with shirts from the thrift store, a pair of white wash jeans, and one pair of dusty red and white Chuck Taylors that I cherished—the only name brand thing that I owned.

The first fight that I ever had in life was over those dirty, old tennis shoes. I'll never forget it. I was fourteen years old, and I lay sleeping in one of the bunk beds at the foster home I was transferred to because of my bad temper and constant fighting. I already knew the day would come that one of the other girls would try me. It never failed. Foster homes were no different from jail or a detention center. Somebody always had to "pull your hoe card," to see if they could run you or not, and I wasn't anybody's bitch. I guess that's just the way it was when you crowded a house with a bunch of problematic children and teens. There were six of us in Ms. Weston's place and lucky me, I got to share a room with Tanisha.

Ms. Weston's house was a pale-yellow, one-story living space. There was one window in every room and she made sure they were covered with bars on the outside, because she had runaways before. It was the only house on the street with bars over the windows. It made everybody look at us funny. For the most part, it was a decent house: five bedrooms, two and a half bathrooms, a kitchen, a dining area, a living room, and a washroom. Ms. Weston kept it pretty clean to say there were a total of eight people living there.

Tanisha was a slob and she always got us into trouble with her method of cleaning, which was simply pushing everything under her bed. She always left water bottles and food plates lying around on the floor. With her trash and funky shoes, by the end of the night, our room smelled like open ass and onions.

Tanisha Watkins was the ugliest broad I'd ever seen in my life—a mixed chick, and whatever nationalities decided to procreate for her existence had gotten it all wrong. She was that nineties-jokes kind of ugly: you so ugly, yo' mama had to feed you with a slingshot; you so ugly, you gotta sneak up to the mirror. I was convinced that being ugly had to be the reason her parents gave her up. I definitely wouldn't want the responsibility of building the confidence of that broad for the next eighteen years. Her skin was light and covered in red bumps and freckles; sometimes you couldn't tell the difference in the two.

On top of being ugly, she was noticeable no matter the distance. She was so knocked-kneed that you could spot her walking anywhere because she looked as if she was walking in circles around herself. On top of the waddling walk she had, she carried at least 190 pounds with her five-foot-three frame, and a head covered in frizzy hair.

Everything about her annoyed me and she had the nerve to further aggravate me with the constant popping of gum.

Like most bullies, Tanisha had an entourage. There must have been some cardinal rule to being a badass: be ugly and have at least two flunkies.

Alexa DeWolfe and Marion Warlow were those two idiots. They followed her everywhere that she went. Alexa was Canadian and in my opinion, she only nipped at the heels of Tanisha because she was the only girl of another race in the house. She'd much rather be a "yes girl" than get her ass kicked every day. Marion was just an idiot. She did all of Tanisha's homework and met every demand as though they were lesbian lovers.

"Bring me some water!" Tanisha would yell.

And like the slave that Marion was, she'd hop up and get it. "You want it with a cup of ice?"

I was about to give everybody in that house a reason to think for themselves.

Tanisha crept beside my little, twin bed one night—the same type of bed that was perfectly uniformed in every room—and tugged at my duffle bag, not exactly being as quiet as she thought she was. I opened one eye and watched her as she rummaged through it and pulled out my red and white sneakers. She smiled, showing crooked teeth. I balled my fist beneath the blanket, which barely reached my feet, and socked her ass with a right hook before she could stand. That one lick probably echoed through all of Junction City, Kansas as she rocked backwards. I knew it had to when the other four girls ran into our bedroom to watch the fight that was about to go down.

4

I jumped out of my bed to give her the ass whipping she'd never get from a parent. Somebody had to teach this heifer a lesson in life—thou shalt not steal. She tried her best to swing her flabby arms at me, but everybody knows that once your back is to the ground and someone is mounting you, your chances of winning are slim to none. I kicked her ass good. With all my might, I attempted to knock a lot more than some sense into her. Our foster mother rushed into the room due to the commotion of the other girls, now awakened loud-whispering, and cheering me on. I didn't even feel the need to talk to her as I whipped her ass—the blows to her head said it all: "I bet. Not catch. You touching. My stuff. Again!" My fist was dialogue enough for the message I put across for her and anybody else that wanted to take something from me.

Ms. Weston lifted me from the floor as I continued to swing. I bit down on my bottom lip—shit just got real face. She carried me to the little office she had in her extra room and tossed me into a big leather chair.

"Calm your little ass down!" she screamed, stress lines wrinkled her forehead.

Ms. Weston looked a bit young to be a foster mother, but I knew she wasn't since she had a grown son. He didn't come around often, but his face was plastered in frames, on walls, and mantels all through the house.

Ms. Weston kept herself up nicely. She was always dressed well, wore very little make-up, and maintained manicured nails. She had a pretty coconut complexion and the weight she carried was simply from age and not laziness. She was always up and moving about, even when she thought everyone was sleeping.

I would watch her from the window as she crept out of the house on the weekends with her purse dangling from her shoulder and her heels click clacking down the walkway.

As I sat slumped down in the chair in her office, she went into a spill on my history of foster homes and the reasons nobody ever wanted me. Her words went in one ear and out the other since I was still fuming about my shoes.

When you didn't have much, you cherished the little bit that you received and anything in that duffle bag was mine; I appreciated it. That duffle bag was my motivation for more, and to this day, I think about it every night as I slide my ass down a pussy-recycled pole for drooling men.

T wo

Dallas, Texas

My hair brushed the floor and I eased down the pole with my clear stilettos pointed toward the roof. The song was ending and my back pressed against the cold stage. One of my regulars, a bowlegged, country white boy, dropped a few more singles on me.

"Thanks, Chad," I said and winked, rolling over to lift myself up and collect my money.

"Give it up for, Siren!" The DJ echoed through the club as I made my exit. Nobody ever really clapped though; might have been a strange action for a strip club, when the only clapping that should be happening was ass cheeks.

One of the strippers, Kitty, my friend, grabbed a handful of my ass when I headed to the dressing room to pack up, since I was done for the night.

"I told you about grabbing my ass!" I yelled over the bass as she followed me into the quiet.

Kitty was the first friend I ever made, ever. She was at the club the first day that I auditioned for Rick, the club owner. She stood leaned against the bar as I did my amateur moves on the pole. Unlike Texas, most cities in Kansas had one strip club. There wasn't much you could learn. The exceptions with more than one but less than five were Wichita, Topeka, Lawrence, and Junction City—where I once resided.

As soon as I stepped down, I was hired instantly. Before I left, she approached me.

"You did your thing up there."

"Thanks," I said, walking away.

"I'm not sure those moves will get you paid though."

I stopped moving my feet. "*I* thought my moves were cash worthy."

"I didn't say you would get nothing. You might walk out with three hundred."

"Three hundred is cool with me."

"Cool if you live somewhere like Galveston. You're in the third largest city in Texas, sweetie. You can rack up."

"And just who are you?" I asked still keeping my distance.

"Cynthia." She extended her hand all politely and shit. "In here, I'm Kitty."

"Siren." I shook only the tips of her fingers.

Kitty offered to show me a few moves. I wasn't used to women being nice to me without wanting something or secretly hating me. They hung around

8

because men favored my looks and flocked to me and I never called a single one friend.

Marion was the first to pretend she was my friend. Once I gave Tanisha the beating of her life, she just didn't seem worthy enough to follow. Marion rushed up behind me as I stepped on to the school bus and joined me in a seat. She complimented my dingy clothes and made small talk about Tanisha, saying how much she hated her.

By our junior year, Marion hated me too, because she realized that although boys flocked to me that didn't mean they'd want to know who my friend was. I never liked any of them anyway, but that didn't matter. Her jealously had festered too long and dug too deep for her to see the truth. She joined the rest of the girls in the house that steered clear of me and by the end of summer she was pregnant. She'd finally found a boy that would give her the time of day.

Because of that situation alone, I started giving girls six months and just as I'd suspect, their shady side would come out of hiding and the "friendship" ended before it even started.

For the first month, I was cautious around Kitty, watching what I said and did, but I learned quickly that Kitty had the same problem with females that I did.

I took a break in the dressing room and Kitty headed upstairs. She wasn't out of site for two seconds when this stripper named Dior started running her mouth.

"I can't stand that hoe," she mentioned to another stripper. "You know she fucked Louis."

"You're lying. I thought Kitty was a dike." The other stripper fed the fire.

"Yeah, when it's convenient for her. Louis is always telling me how she sucked him off. He said she wasn't even that *fye* at giving head." She laughed.

I knocked something to the floor purposely and they both looked in my direction and turned up their noses.

"Oh, my bad. Did I interrupt your simple bitch conversation?"

"What you said?"

"You heard me. Can't y'all find nothing else to discuss other than somebody who not in the room to hear that stupid shit y'all talking?"

"Oh no this hoe didn't."

I don't know why I felt the need to defend Kitty. I guess I'd had enough experience in foster care with females like that, always standing in the shadows with their rumors and opinions and never woman enough to approach you and tell you straight up that they don't like you.

"I did. You standing there talking about somebody when all you are is a cracked-out, stank pussy stripper. Why you think all the customers get up when you bring your rancid ass on stage? Go wash your ass before you *drag* for somebody who doesn't give two fucks about you."

Dior would have snapped back had her buddy not laughed. Instead, she stormed out of the dressing room and she never said another thing around me.

They only hated Kitty because she was beautiful. So beautiful that she could be the ninth wonder of the world even though an eighth had yet to be officially listed, only referred. Kitty had runway legs carrying her five-foot-nine physique. Her body was *Insanity* workout fit and her ass was stacked behind her, rumbling with every step.

Unlike Tanisha, the attempted shoe thief, Kitty was a flawless bi-racial mix: a white-American father and a Black-Jamaican mother. Every good trait that her parents had, she got: a twenty-six inch waist, flawless skin, a tiny pointed nose, and perky breasts to complete her perfect package. Yeah, I looked. So what? We stripped for a living. Her baby face and bangs were added bonuses to her banging body, which kept the men drooling. They handed over their whole paycheck just to be in her presence, but like the simple bitch said, Kitty fancied the other sex.

My mouth dropped the first time that the dike rumor was confirmed. I saw her in a black Ranger Rover, tonguing some girl down and squeezing her nipples through a barely there shirt. She looked up at me and winked then went right back to what she was doing. I had never really been exposed to that type of lifestyle, and I had seen a lot of shit before I even hit age eleven.

Kitty came to me the next day as if I hadn't seen her with a girl. She teased me about the expression that was on my face and told me her story. She never liked men. The only man that ever touched her was her daddy—her real one—but he paid for that with a knife in his back when her older brother, Corey, caught him trying to stick his bird in a nest it didn't build. Her brother was still in jail until this day. You had to love the American justice system and I mean that with as much sarcasm as possible.

She even cleared up the rumor about Louis, the simple bitch's boyfriend. He wanted to talk to her, but when she rejected him, he told Dior things that weren't true to create a rift between them.

Kitty never knew her mom. She'd seen a few pictures of her and she knew her name—Laurie— but she didn't know what they had in common. She wished that she knew her but that's all that it was a wish. I figured one of two was wonderful, even if her father did touch her. I knew zero. Didn't even have a picture.

Kitty and I spent every moment together in and out of the strip club. Even if she was fucking some girl, I was in the next room. I'd read books or watch something foolish on television. At the time, my obsession was reruns of Charmed.

We stayed up late nights talking about our past, fears, failures, and future. For the first time I opened up to someone. She made it easy. I told her everything, even my real name. My real, real name and not the ones I made up when meeting strangers who refused to accept my stage name as legit. I could tell her anything, because I knew she'd take it to her grave, secret or not. If it wasn't for her friendship, after six months, I would have been on to the next city. I'd already lived in five other cities.

I considered her the sister I never had, an older/wiser one, since she was always lecturing me and telling me what to do with my life and my money—as if she wasn't the same age as me: twenty-one. "You need to have a plan, Siren, you can't strip all your life" was her favorite line.

Kitty was in college, double majoring in psychology and criminal justice. She wanted to defend the innocent, accused guilty—people like her brother.

"I can't help it. I see ass and I have to touch it." Kitty smiled.

"Gay ass."

"And proud of it," she laughed. "You need to hop on over to this side and let me show you how to really live. You have the perfect lips for eating pussy." She eyed my kissers.

"Quit looking at my mouth, freak."

She giggled. "So, where you headed after this?"

"To get a room and some sleep."

"You still haven't found a place, yet?"

"I'm not looking."

"Girl, you bank a 'G' or more every night. You know how many twenty-one year olds wish they made that much? You can find somewhere nicer than those hotels you crashing in."

"I prefer a hotel rather than handing over a ridiculous amount of money for property I'll never own, and besides, my clock is running out in this city. I'm ready to try some place new," I confessed as I threw my jeans and t-shirt on.

"Oh, you're trying to leave me? At least let me fuck first," she taunted. "You say that shit every night. You're not leaving me."

I pulled my thong from my body and tossed it at Kitty's face and she caught them. "That's the closest you'll ever get to this na-na."

She lifted them to her nose and took a whiff. "Mm, that just made me want you even more."

I laughed. "Nasty, bitch." I packed up my bag and tossed it over my shoulder. "Are you still doing my hair tomorrow?"

"I got you, boo. Stay until my shift ends and sleep at my place tonight. I wish you would just move in."

"Cool. Give me your keys so I can put my bag in your truck. And moving in with you would be the same as paying rent. Leave me be."

Kitty handed me the keys from her bag and I left. She grabbed my ass one more time and ran off before I could smack her.

T hree

"I swear you make me sick with all this hair on your damn head," Kitty said as she braided my hair back.

"Jealous, are we?" I teased.

"Hell yeah, I'm jealous. You have hair down your back and you keep it under a wig."

"It's too difficult to manage."

"I manage it just fine. Some girls would kill for all this hair. Shit, they'd kill just to look like you."

Even though I didn't know my parents, there was one thing I was sure of: they were attractive and I got all their best features. Everywhere that I went, girls envied me. I had naturally long lashes, Naomi Campbell cheekbones, and Meagan Good lips. For most of my life, people always complimented me, telling me how beautiful I was (for a black girl), and that I could easily be a model. Don't think that the "black" comment didn't bother me. I gave them the blues for that statement. Black was beautiful no matter what shade.

I took my face and body as an apology from God for the life he gave me. I could hear him saying, "Sorry you don't have parents, but at least you're beautiful."

Poor Tanisha Watkins.

"Can I ask you something?" Kitty asked.

"I guess so."

"Where the hell are you from?"

I shrugged my shoulders.

"You don't know where you're from?" Shock rang in her voice.

"I was told Mississippi, but I don't ever remember being there."

"I'm confused."

"I grew up in foster care."

"That explains a lot. How come you never told me that before? I mean, I know that you didn't know you're parents, so I assumed that you lived with an aunt or another family member."

"I wish. It would have been better than growing up with complete strangers. And what do you mean by that explains a lot?"

"No offense, but Siren, you got issues."

"No, I don't."

"Psshh, yes, you do. You do inventory on all your shit every night. You damn near broke Starr's arm for borrowing your brush. And, you refuse to move into an apartment or buy a car. That has commitment and abandonment issues written all over it. You refuse to take responsibility for anything."

"Are you diagnosing me? Damn psychology majors."

"It's the truth. I can't even figure you out. We've been friends for what… a year and some days now? When we go out to eat, you never order the same thing twice. Everybody has a favorite something or at least a little routine. Nothing about you stays the same."

"I guess."

"Don't get defensive. I'm just calling it like I see it. And now you're talking about moving."

"I'm moving because I need a change of scenery and more money."

"A *G* a night is good money. You don't spend it on nothing but food, costumes, and hotels."

"Shit, the strippers down in Atl make way more than that. I'm trying to get on that level. I can spend it on whatever I want."

"So money is your only motivation in life?"

"Pretty much. I don't have kids or a husband. What else is there to do other than make sure I'm taken care of day-to-day? You only get one life, might as well make sure you have the best of everything while you're here."

"There is more to life than material things. And *again*, you don't buy anything!" Kitty emphasized.

"This, coming from a stripper, who drags me to the mall for Michael Kors bags and Chanel anything. And there isn't anything I want to buy right now. I'm saving it. I don't know for what yet. I'm just saving it."

"Hey, I like nice things, but I want love and kids too, so we can all have nice things together. You? You're saving for yourself."

"Bitch, you can't have kids. You like women."

"Men do still exist, you know. I don't need his dick, just his sperm. Everything in me still works," she said and popped me on top of my head with the rattail comb. "I'm finished. Grab your shit so we can get to this club."

Kitty handed me her keys. "You drive. Maybe driving my whip will make you feel on top of the world and you'll go out and get your own," she teased.

"Forget you. I don't need a car. Maybe I'll just pay you to be my chauffer and change your name to Alfred."

"That's a man's name."

"Aren't you the man in your relationships?" I got up to run out of the house and she chased me. "Come, come, Alfred." I laughed aloud and we got into the car.

It had only been a few weeks that I had my driver's license. Kitty was shocked and appalled to learn that I couldn't drive, so she made it her business to teach me. I didn't care for it much, but I loved how excited Kitty was about having someone to teach.

After a few minutes, we stopped at a gas station close to the club so she could get a pack of Black and Mild cigars. I hated those things. I was more of a drinker than a smoker.

"Get me a drink!" I yelled through the passenger side window as Kitty headed into the store. I sat tapping my fingers against the steering wheel as music blared from the speakers. She emerged after five minutes and we were on our way to the club. I sipped on the coke she got me then sat it in the cup holder.

"Can I tell you something and you not get all weird?" Kitty asked.

"Just tell me."

"You're the best friend I've ever had, Siren, and I love you."

I felt a twinge of something in my body, something I couldn't explain. Nobody had ever said those words to me. I pulled up to a red light and faced her, wanting to look her in the eyes with my reply. "I love you, too," I responded with ease and meant it.

Kitty returned my smile and just as she opened her mouth to speak, the glasses behind us shattered. We both screamed. I ducked my head down. Shots fired into the car and boys yelled. The only line I caught was, "That's not his truck!" and then feet scrambled. I lifted my head up in a panic. Kitty was slumped over. I reached for her to check her, but there was no response as I pushed at her.

"Kitty," I said calmly at first then yelled when I noticed her shirt soaked in blood. "Kitty!" I screamed and jumped out of the truck to pull her from the other side. A car pulled up behind us and turned on their hazard lights.

"Help me! Help me!" I cried as I rocked Kitty and tapped her face, hoping she was just unconscious and not dead. Shattered glass pushed into my skin. People rushed over, but I couldn't be moved no matter how many people tugged at me. I couldn't speak no matter how many people asked me a question.

"Kitty!" I wailed out into the night sky. My chest was tight and I could barely breathe. This can't be happening.

"Kitttyyyyy!"

Right at that moment, I vowed never to get behind a wheel again.

F_{our}

Kitty, Cynthia Mass, had only been gone a week, and I wasn't making it without her. If this was what it felt like to love somebody and lose them, then I didn't want shit else to do with the feeling. I still saw her in my arms, lifeless, eyes wide open. I threw back Patron shots to kill the image.

I hadn't even bothered to take the next night off. I needed more money so I could get the fuck out of Dallas. Being a stripper didn't grant me bereavement anyway, so I had to work.

I sat with a piece of paper and an ink pen in front of me at my station. It had Kitty's brother's name written at the top of it. Somebody had to tell him she was gone. She was all he had.

It broke my heart to walk around her apartment and see all the pictures of her and her brother as kids hanging against her wall. The good always die young. She kept all of his letters in a drawer in her bedroom. I grabbed one just to get his address and the rest I burned before her nosey ass extended family could come and read them and take anything of value.

She didn't have an insurance policy, so I paid for her funeral with some of the money I had saved up. All of her regular customers came, the family she never spoke to, and a few of her ex-girlfriends. Everybody cried—the real and the fake but not me. I was still in disbelief that it really happened.

I took a recent picture of her from her apartment and tucked it into my duffel bag with my red and white sneakers. Yes, I still had them. Now she was in the bag of items that meant everything to me.

"Siren, we need you on the floor," a woman's voice called.

"In a minute!" I yelled toward the door, not bothering to turn to see who it was.

I abandoned the pen and paper and headed out to the club. I walked over to the bar for another shot. I could feel all eyes on me, all sympathy stares. Everybody knew Kitty and I were thick as thieves. A cold hand patted me on my back and I turned.

"Hey, Chad," I said.

"Hey, beautiful. Sorry about your loss."

"Thanks." I forced a smile.

"I heard it was your last night at the club. If there is anything that I can do for you before you leave, just let me know."

The bartender handed me my shot and I threw it back. "Actually, there is. I need a ride to the airport in the morning. I was just going to call a taxi, but sometimes they can be kind of slow."

"Just give me a time and I'm there." He smiled.

"Darlene, can I get a pen?" I yelled over the bar and pulled one of the small, white, square napkins from the wooden holster. I jotted down the address to the hotel I was staying at and my flight time. "Thanks, Chad."

He gave me a wink and placed the napkin into his pocket. I walked away to make some last minute cash.

I didn't even bother going to sleep. It would make much sense with the hours that I worked. I went straight from the club to my room to sit and wait. I had the first flight to Louisiana booked. It wasn't that far, but it was away from where I was.

Chad called my room phone to see if I was ready. All I had was my duffle bag. It was all that I ever needed.

"Good morning, beautiful." Chad smiled.

"Morning," I said and eased into his passenger side, tossing my bag behind his seat.

"Which airport you going to?"

"Love."

"Alright, buckle up," he said and pulled off.

I entertained him with idle conversation as he drove. Dallas was so damn spread out; I figured that I might as well sit back and chitchat.

He told me about his wife and three kids. I was surprised he knew anything about them at all, as much time as he spent at the strip club, tipping me all his money. Chad was never disrespectful though, if there was such a thing as respect in such an environment. Most wives deemed it disrespectful for a man to simply enter a strip club, but wouldn't meet him halfway by stripping for him at home. The way I saw it, strippers only did what they wouldn't. Chad never got loud; he'd have one drink, and toss a generous amount of money. From what he was saying about how wonderful his family was, I couldn't understand why he spent so much time in a strip club, so I asked.

"I love black women" was his response. I laughed. All the white boys do, even the ones that won't admit it. He went on to tell me why he loved black women so much and then I understood what it was that his wife lacked—ass and attitude.

We pulled up to the passenger drop-off and, like a gentleman, Chad hopped out, retrieved my bag from the backseat, and ran around to my side to open my door. Of course, I'd already beat him to the last one. He handed me my bag and I gave him a hug.

"I'm surely going to miss you down at the club."

"I'll miss you too," I said and began walking away.

"Hey," he paused. "What's your name, your real name?"

"Cynthia." I smiled as I added on a new fake alias.

"Call me if you ever need anything, Cynthia."

"Thanks, Chad."

I walked into the airport and stood in line to get my ticket. I didn't have a bankcard so I couldn't conveniently use the kiosk they had available. I only had one bag, so I just carried it on the plane with me. I headed for security and after the ridiculous check, I went to my terminal, grabbing a sandwich from Subway while I waited to board.

I started thinking about Kitty's brother, Corey. I needed to write him and tell him that she was gone. Kitty told me one night while we were sharing our tales of past and present, that he wouldn't answer letters from anyone but her. Their family had turned their back on them after the death of their father and only called when they needed something. So, if ever anyone wrote him, he tossed their letter in the trash. I had already labeled the envelope with Kitty's name and address. It was time I actually wrote the letter.

I remember wondering why they wrote and didn't call one another, but Kitty cleared that up by telling me that it was his preference. The phone calls were too short for all that he wanted to say. He wanted something he could keep and also offered unlimited conversation.

I apologized to him for being misleading and said that I wouldn't have done it if it wasn't necessary. I hated that I had to be the bearer of bad news. I told him that, too. It was challenging to deliver such news, but I knew that it was much more difficult for him to receive. I hoped that when he read the letter that he was sitting down. *"Cynthia is dead"* was somewhere on the sixth line of the page and I figured by then he just might stop reading. I hoped the word dead wasn't too harsh. I couldn't imagine what he felt sitting in a room with all his rights stripped, being treated like an animal for killing his father, and now having to learn that his sister was gone too. There was a possibility that he'd ball the paper up and toss it at the wall. He'd hate me for not saying something sooner. I hadn't known that prisoners could go to the funerals of immediate family members, so like the police, I'd violated him of a right.

I told him the answer to what I assumed would be his first question. *"She was shot and killed as we left a gas station and the police wrote it up as mistaken identity."* I went on to tell him that the police had no leads and unfortunately, I didn't get a look at a single suspect. That part was a bit much.

I then explained who I was and how I knew Kitty. *"She was my best friend, my only,"* I said. I apologized for taking so long to send the letter; I, too, was all messed up and didn't know my left from my right, but if he needed someone to hate, it could be me.

In closing, I let him know that she was properly buried and that I loved Kitty, to him, Cynthia, like a sister. I claimed him as my brother. If she loved him, then I guess I loved him too. And in loving him, I took on the responsibility of keeping money on his books and sending him a letter to keep him in touch with the outside world. He was all that I had left of Kitty, even if I didn't know him well. I knew what I was told and that was admirable. I gave him the option of writing me back by letting him know that wherever I was, I would get a P.O. Box. It was then that I informed him of my floating habits. I apologized for his loss once more then signed and sealed the letter to be sent off immediately.

Five

New Orleans, Louisiana

I closed my eyes only for a second and dozed off without realizing it. When I opened them back up, I was in New Orleans, Louisiana: the city of spicy foods, fast-talking, jazz music, and graves above ground. I smiled as the flight attendant welcomed us and told us to prepare for landing. My heart was still heavy, but at least I was in a new place to clear my head.

It took me all of two minutes to gather myself and exit the plane before everybody else. I exited the terminal and read the signs to the exit. I had some things I needed to handle.

The humid air of New Orleans hit me and I squinted and fanned the heat. Although, it was hot there, it was much better than the dry heat that I had to bear in Texas.

I walked out front and hopped into the first available taxi. "Closest Best Buy please," I directed.

For the entire ride, the driver watched me in his rearview mirror. I looked up and turned my nose up at him and he looked away, clearing his throat. Didn't anybody tell this motherfucker that staring was rude?

We pulled up to Best Buy and I handed him a few dollars as a tip and asked him to wait. I wasn't paying until my final destination, because cab drivers were some shady people. I took my duffle bag with me. I took it everywhere. I didn't need to look around, I knew exactly what I needed—a phone and laptop. A jolly white girl, with a head full of blue-streaked hair, walked over to me in her blue shirt. She clearly took her job too seriously.

"May I help you with something?"

"I need to get a phone."

"Alright, follow me."

She started rattling off all these different brands and their features. She asked me if I preferred Samsung, Ericsson and some other irrelevant brands; they all did the same things, right? I tilted my head to the side because I honestly didn't know the difference. I really didn't care; I just needed it to dial out and receive calls. I wanted to keep my promises to Corey and these two things would help me do that.

After about thirty minutes, the associate realized I wasn't into anything fancy that she was selling. She sold me a regular, flip prepaid phone since I didn't have many people to call. I grabbed the laptop without her help. I paid and returned to my taxi. He was still there.

"Take me to a post office then to wherever downtown is," I instructed.

"Any place in particular downtown?"

"Anywhere near Bourbon."

He nodded and pulled off. No matter what cities I traveled to, I knew all downtown areas had two things: strip clubs and hotels.

I didn't know much about New Orleans, except for the things I read growing up. Kitty talked about it all the time, because she once dated a girl who lived here. She always joked that the girl put voodoo on her, because it was the only time in her life that she was actually faithful. She said her New Orleans' girl was the reason she yearned for love and the family life, but she also said the bitch was crazy. She loved to hate her.

Kitty always talked about Bourbon Street. She said the locals didn't find much about it exciting, but she loved it. She bragged about the Cherry Bombs and Hand Grenades, the strip clubs, restaurants, gift shops, and local accents. She was fascinated with the fact that the further you walked down Bourbon Street, the gayer it turned. Rainbow flags hung from buildings; drag queens, and half-naked men stood in the middle of the street talking, drinking, and making out. To her, that was living.

The cabby pulled up to the post office. It took me five minutes inside, and I retrieved the form I needed for a P.O. Box. I hopped back into the yellow taxi and the driver dropped me at the corner of St. Charles and Canal, which wasn't far from the post office he had just taken me to on a street named Loyola.

"Where's Bourbon?" I asked.

"Just cross the street and the name changes. You're on Bourbon."

I paid him and slid out, Best Buy bag in hand and duffle on my shoulder. I looked around at the tall buildings and the people crossing the street whether the light was red or not. Horns honked, taxis blocked lanes, and police cars drove up and down in the middle of two-way traffic. I fell into the crowd as groups crossed over.

Bourbon didn't seem that fascinating in daylight, but there were sites that made me smile: the man playing the trumpet, kids tap dancing with tennis shoes, and a woman selling roses from a cart. Looked like a city of hustlers, which meant I was in the right place.

I moved further up the street and almost passed out from the loud smell of shit, piss, sewage, and whatever else. I covered my nose, while others around me didn't even seem fazed by the stench.

I entered into the first strip club that I saw. It was on the right hand side and girls danced in the window. One licked her tongue at me and I laughed. Nobody sat at the front door so I just headed in.

"Can I do something for you?" A male's voice said through dim light.

"I'm looking for the owner or manager."

"You have an appointment?"

"No, are you the manager?"

"Depends on who's asking."

I followed the sound of his voice and met him halfway around the stage in the middle of the floor. He smiled when he saw my face and looked me up and down.

"Damn," he said, not bothering to hide his thoughts. That was a man's favorite word when seeing me. It was old now.

I wasn't even sure what he was saying damn to when my hair was still in the week old braids that Kitty put them in. I rocked a pair of ripped jeans and a beater and that, to me, wasn't flattering.

"Let me guess," he said looking me up and down. "Dancer?"

I nodded my head.

"You trying to audition?"

"If you have room for me."

"I can never have enough dancers. Can you work a pole? Because if you can't, don't even waste my time or yours. I can point you to She-She's or something. Our customers like skill here. Any average hoe can shake their ass."

"I'm definitely not average." I smirked.

"Show me what you got then." He stepped out of the way.

Thanks to Kitty, who was a pole dancing extraordinaire, I had skills that were unmatched. She taught me everything I knew. I kicked off my shoes and dropped my jeans right there, sitting my things on a vacant chair. I was far from shy.

I hopped up on stage and went straight for the pole, climbing to the top and tricking all the way down. No music played, but I didn't need it as 'Skin' by Rihanna played in my head. It was Kitty's favorite pole-dancing song. I ended the little routine in a split and when I looked up, the manager's mouth was wide open.

"You are bad, girl. I wasn't expecting that. Can you start tonight?"

"I can start whenever you want me to."

"I like that. Be here for ten."

He handed me his card: Gerald Poinson, Manager. I tucked the card into my bag and slipped back into my jeans and shoes. I needed to get a room and a new costume since I left all my old things behind. Starting over never bothered me.

Bourbon was a different street when I returned, a band played on the corner and people danced in the street. Cars tried to drive down but were forced to turn off so people could walk wherever they wanted. Now I was starting to see the hype.

I walked into the club and the bouncer smiled. "It's a ten dollar cover, love," he said.

"I'm dancing here."

"Oh, you're the new chick everybody can't wait to see."

Word traveled fast. The guard stood and escorted me through the club to Gerald's office.

"You look like a different person from earlier, still fine as ever, but different," Gerald said as he stood from his desk.

I didn't doubt that I looked different since after leaving the club, I booked a room and started prepping myself for the night. I finally cried for Kitty and I unraveled my braids and let my crinkled hair hang past my shoulders. I tweezed my brows and did my makeup. I was ready to work that stage and make some fools come up out of their hard-earned cash.

"Thank you, I guess," I smiled.

"Have a seat."

I took a seat in front of him and he rattled off the rules, which were very simple: no prostituting and to pay him his percentage of my tips. He told me I had a week to prove I was worth keeping around and then he entertained me with stories of strippers that he'd fired in the past. *How the fuck does a stripper get fired?*

Apparently, it happens. Only a few weeks ago, he had to let a stripper go for pick pocketing the customers, and another one, weeks before that for selling weed and pills on the property.

"Come on. Let me introduce you to the girls." He stood.

I stood too and followed, ready for whatever was about to come my way.

"You have a stage name already?" he asked.

"Yeah, Siren."

"Cool."

We walked to the back and there were naked bitches everywhere. He got everyone's attention to introduce me. Some girls smiled and others rolled their eyes. He was loose in calling them bitches and hoes—nothing new. There were no ladies in this industry.

My eyes followed his pointed finger as he told me who everybody was. You had Princess, a short thick bitch with a butterfly tattoo on her ass and a septum piercing. Nicki Minaj was clearly her idol from the looks of the pink lipstick and bleach blonde wig, which was not at all flattering to her dark skin.

Next, there was Cherry. She was tall and her hair was faded and dyed red, her legs were covered with black stars and her cheeks were pierced. Bitch, if God didn't give you dimples, you weren't meant to have them. I'm just saying.

"That's Heaven." He pointed. "Heaven. Heaven, turn around."

"For what? This bitch ain't special. You come back here introducing this hoe like she a celebrity

35

or some shit. Quit fronting like this some shit you been doing."

All the girls laughed.

Gerald was clearly afraid of Heaven. I made the assumption that she was fucking him from his body language. She could talk to him stupid, but she damn sure wasn't about to disrespect me.

"I clearly mean something if he felt the need to change his routine," I snapped.

"Excuse me?" she said and finally turned to face us. Heaven matched me in height. Her back was covered in colorful flowers and unlike the rest of the strippers; her face was free of piercings. Ignorant bitch or not, she was gorgeous. Her hair was jet black and hung around her shoulders, parted up the middle. "Bitch you don't know me."

"And you don't know me," I said, dropping my bag on the floor. I was ready to roll with this bitch if need be. The room was silent.

"Alright, chill out. Heaven, get your ass out front."

She smirked and slid her feet into her stilettos then walked past me, bumping my shoulder. I thought to knock her ass over, but it was my first night, and I needed to get my stacks back up after paying for a funeral. I'd handle beef later. Bitch hated me for no reason, but I was used to that.

S ix

I sat in front of the mirror in the dressing room, lining my eyes. I hated mirrors and not because I hated to look at myself. Mirrors reminded me of Ms. Weston. After my first fight, I started to look at her as a real mother figure. She lectured me all night that night; told me that I was too pretty to let ugly girls upset me. She asked me if I wanted to get kicked out of another foster home and I shook my with my arms folded across my chest.

"Just do what I say and we both can make it through the days to come," she said and sent me back to my bed.

I shadowed her after that, drinking in her knowledge and lying for her whenever facilitators came to inspect the home. They had heard the rumors of her late night creeps and abandoning us. Not to mention, the male company she had over often. It was never the same guy twice. I told them different, batting my eyelashes and showing my best smile.

Ms. Weston would always stand behind me in the mirror, telling me how pretty I was as she styled my hair and thanked me for what I did. For a moment, I actually thought she loved me and it made me feel good to know I was capable of being loved.

She gave me things: hair products, jewelry, clothes, shoes, etc. All in private and she told me not to show the other girls because they would get jealous. She also made sure I didn't have another problem out of Tanisha by having her moved to another foster home with the help of false documentation. I was special. That's what she said. I was special.

On many occasions, she promised to get me information about my real parents and that motivated me to keep up the scams.

A week before my eighteenth birthday, she came to me as I separated the pretty curls she rolled into my hair.

"Come see me in my office when you're done," *she instructed.*

I skipped to her office and tapped on the door before entering.

"Come in," she said, clearing her throat. *"Have a seat."*

I sat before her.

"I wanted to talk to you. You know you're due for release when you turn eighteen."

I nodded.

"What are your plans?"

"I'm not exactly sure."

"How would you feel if I asked you to stick around and help me out?"

"Around the home?"

"Not exactly." She stood up and walked over to the door that I forgot to close. She pushed it and locked it. "I need a favor."

"What kind of favor?"

"Now, I wouldn't ask you to do this unless I really needed to, but I already said you'd do it."

"What is it?"

She moved to sit back down behind her desk. "I have a problem. I've had it for years and this time, I may have gone a bit too far. I lost my house. I can get it back, but..."

"What does that have to do with me?" I asked, getting agitated with her long explanation for this favor.

"My son bought the house at the auction and he'll give it back to me if I can make payments."

"I don't have any money, Ms. Weston, and why won't your son just give it back to you? That's your family."

She sighed. "I bought this house after my husband died and it's the only thing I ever had for myself. Now it's in my son's name and as long as it's in his name, he'll want me to follow his rules like I'm his child and not his mother. I refinanced it trying to save my car. Everything is all messed up." She looked down then back up at me with a broken look in her eyes. "I told him you'd offer your services. Help out at his club to pay off the debt. I only make enough to take care of this house and you girls."

Did she say club? My eyes lit up at the naive idea of maybe serving drinks or collecting money at the door. I'd always wanted to be like the bartenders I saw on television, tossing glasses around and shit.

"I'll be happy to help, Ms. Weston." She smiled and rushed around to hug me tight. "When do I start?" I asked.

"On your birthday, because you have to be eighteen."

The day of my birthday rolled around and Ms. Weston took extra special care of me. She got me a hotel room and made several appointments for my hair, nails, feet, and body waxing. I thought it was her way of saying thank you for doing her this favor.

We pulled up to her son's club that night and she smiled and looked over at me, telling me to ask for Barry then speeding off when I stepped out. I yelled for her, but she kept on going. I walked up to the front door and the bouncer smiled at me. "You must be the new girl."

"I guess so. Is Barry here?"

"Yeah, he's sitting at the bar. You can't miss him. He's in all white."

Barry sat at the bar, one foot propped up and the other pressed to the floor. I shook my head. Who does he think he is, Diddy? *I tapped him on*

40

*the shoulder and he turned as if he wanted to hit
me, but quickly caught himself and blinked several
times. "Damn. My mama said you were beautiful."*

*His compliment made me uncomfortable. It
wasn't until he complimented me that I noticed the
half-naked woman behind the bar and the single
pole sticking up through the small stage. It
reflected beneath the neon lights and was only big
enough to do a two-step on.*

*Barry looked just like his mother: same
complexion, same wide nose and mouth, and stress
lines in his forehead. He was nothing special.*

*"Come on, let's get you set up," he said and
gulped his drink until none was left.*

*I followed him to his office and he pulled out a
bag and started digging through it. "Since it's your
first night, I'll provide your costumes. I'll be taking
fifty percent—"*

"Wait, what do I need a costume for?"

He stopped and looked up. "To dance."

*"Dance? I thought I was going to be
bartending or something."*

*"In Kansas?" he laughed. "Gotta be twenty-
one to do that sweetheart."*

"I didn't come here to strip."

*He laughed again. "I guess my mama only
gave you half the job description."*

"She didn't give me any of it," I snapped.

*He shook his head. "Look, you're throwing
that attitude in the wrong direction. I know your
situation. You don't have anywhere else to go. You*

41

got two minutes to decide if you want to make some money or go find a comfortable spot on the sidewalk, because I can guarantee my mama won't answer your calls. That's how she works. Why do you think I'm making her pay me? She uses everyone to her own benefit. My daddy never even wanted her with that house. He knew she'd run it into the ground."

Ms. Weston played me. I stood there in silence, uncomfortable, and with my back against a wall. I didn't have a penny to my name and no place to sleep. All the love I thought I was receiving from Ms. Weston was just preparation for me to be pimped out at her benefit. It made me happy that she thought she was dealing with a young dummy.

"Alright, I'll dance, but I want to work a new deal."

"I'm listening."

"I'll dance for free, but I want the deed to that house."

Barry smiled a sinister smile. "Guess you aren't as stupid as my mama thought you to be. Don't feel bad though. She's fucked over me more than I can count. You have yourself a deal." He winked and tossed a costume at me. "You need a name."

"For what?"

"All dancers have a stage name." He looked me up and down. "I heard you read a lot. Are you into Greek Mythology?"

"I've read some. I'm an avid reader."

42

"When you get some time, look up Siren, because that's what I think of when I look at you. You are gorgeous, girl."

"What do you know about it? You own a strip club."

"Looks aren't always what they seem, darling. Stick around. You'll learn a thing or two. Now, go get dressed."

Ms. Weston was in for a rude awakening if she thought she was going to use me and toss me out when she was done. I danced until that deed was put in my hands. Only took me eight months and by that time, I was addicted to the lifestyle.

Ms. Weston blew her lid when she realized I wasn't a dummy. I didn't even really know what to do with the deed. I just knew it was a slip of paper that told you who the owner was and now, the owner was me. I got that document in my hand and skipped town. I didn't care what happened to her after that.

Nobody told her to spend all her cash at Prairie Band Casino and Resort.

I didn't have the time to wait for Karma to catch Ms. Weston. I needed it to happen right then.

"Siren, Siren."

"Huh?" I swung around in my chair.

"G wants you to work the floor," Cherry said.

"Okay," I said, setting my eyeliner down on the vanity. Now wasn't the time to be visiting the past. I had money to make.

Seven

I stood in line at the post office, waiting to turn in my paperwork for a P.O. Box and mail off an updated letter to Corey. I'd been so busy sleeping and dancing that I let it slip my mind. I felt bad for forgetting because he could be sitting around waiting with all his questions. I wanted to keep every promise that I made to him.

A tall man, dressed in a business suit, stared at me, while he talked on his cell phone. I wanted to ask what the hell he was looking at, but opted not to, because the post office was no place to cause a scene.

"Next in line, please," an older woman, wearing her glasses at the tip of her nose, said.

People who worked state jobs always looked angry. Even when you were friendly with them, they wore the same expression. I tossed my paperwork on the counter giving her the same *mugged* expression she was giving me. *Bitch, you chose this job. Don't like it then find another one.* If I said half the things I was thinking, I'd be in jail or involved in a lot of physical altercations and arguments.

"How long do you want to reserve it for?" she asked, keeping her eyes on the paperwork.

"Three months," I replied as the tall businessman walked up to the customer service representative beside mine and didn't attempt to hide that he was watching me. He looked me up and down.

Old Grouchy excused herself without saying excuse me, then returned with a key for me and told me to follow her. She showed me my box and we tested the key then walked back inside, so that I could pay. I jotted down the P.O. Box address on the letter to Corey and tossed that to her as well and paid for it. I snatched my key from her hand without a thank you and headed out before dude could stare a hole through me.

Not even a minute later, he ran out behind me. "Hey!"

"Can I help you, sir?"

"What's your name?"

"Why?"

"You look real familiar, but I can pinpoint where I've met you."

"I can't help you. I'm not even from here. You have a good day."

Instead of frowning at my rudeness, he smiled and walked away. I rolled my eyes and went on about my day.

Seven days and already, I was ten thousand dollars richer. Lucky for me, I started the week that the Essence Festival was in town, which meant men with money were all over the city. They stepped into the club buying the bar and dropping stacks on any bad bitch that stepped on stage. No matter where I stood or danced in the club, Heaven had her eyes on me. I usually would wear wigs when I preformed, but knowing that I had Heaven's eyes on me all night, I wore my own hair and swung it around just because I could.

"Can I get a dance, pretty lady?" A deep voice asked from behind me as I leaned against the bar. I pivoted to see the man who was damn near stalking me at the post office. His dark chocolate skin beamed under the neon lights. He still wore his suit and stood with one hand in his pocket and the other grasping the toothpick between his lips.

"Follow me." I said and led him toward the private rooms.

No more words were exchanged as he followed me with a *smoove* walk—yes, *smoove*. He took his seat against the wall and held out twenty dollars in front of me. I pulled it from his hands and tossed it to the floor then began giving him what he came for. I bent over touching my toes and another big face was slid into my thong. I pulled it out and tossed it in front of me. *Hello, Benjamin Franklin.*

"I knew you looked familiar," he said.

"Been here before?" I asked, rolling my stomach.

"I'm here every day, but I always just catch glimpses of you. You're new, right?"

"Yep."

"Where are you from?"

"My mama's womb."

He laughed. "Cute. What's your name?"

"Siren."

"Your real name."

"You pay for the fantasy, baby, not my reality."

"That's fair. Well, Siren, I'd really like to take you out sometime, outside of this place." He tossed another Ben.

"You don't consider this a date?" I said, straddling him.

"No."

"Why not?"

"Because you won't tell me anything about yourself here. I'd like to know your reality."

"Pass," I said, easing from his lap.

"How old are you?" he asked, not giving up.

"Ten, eleven." I finally decided to give him a bit of truth. I continued to dance, not caring to keep up the conversation.

"Don't you want to know anything about me?"

"You're old, you clearly have money, and you stalk women at post offices. I know enough."

He laughed. "I'll wear you down eventually." He tossed more bills.

"You know where to find me."

After a few more tricks, I gathered Ben and his identical twin brothers that totaled out to five-hundred and twenty dollars. I sashayed my ass out of that room, stuffing them into my money bag. Heaven was on her way to the back with a customer and bumped my shoulder as she pulled his hand. I was sick of that bitch.

I marched straight to Gerald's office, not bothering to knock before I entered. "You better get your girl together."

"Huh? Who?"

"Heaven. She has one more time to bump me or look at me stupid, and I'm going to lay her out."

"Sit down. Heaven is just a little intimidated by you. That's all. Before you came in here, she had all the men here sweating her like she was the only chick in the city."

"Including you?"

"Don't overstep," Gerald got defensive.

I wasn't stupid. In a week's time, I'd caught her sucking his dick when he thought nobody was around, arguing in the men's bathroom, and sliding her gifts. To make shit worse, she didn't even pay him a percentage of the tips she got. I wondered how the other dancers would feel about that.

"I'm not overstepping shit."

"Yeah, you are." He licked his lips. "My mind not even on no Heaven. I got my sites set elsewhere." He bit his bottom lip.

"I hope you aren't referring to me."

"And if I am?"

"Then you need to press reset," I said and stood to leave.

"I could make you a real star!" he yelled to my back as I headed to the dressing room. I shook my head and went to change.

I walked over to my locker and the lock had been broken. Heat rose through my body instantly, and I swung it open to see my bag missing. Not thinking, I turned to face the other girls. They all looked like Tanisha to me and would be getting a matching ass whipping if my shit didn't turn up.

"Where's my bag?!" I asked angrily and they all laughed. "This isn't a fucking joke. Who broke my lock and took my bag?"

Nobody said anything, but Heaven's two goons, Cocoa and Trixie, were laughing enough to let me know who the culprit was. I slammed the door to the locker and stomped to the private room where Heaven entertained her customer. I grabbed her shoulder, turning her around and began decking her in the face. The client stood to stop the fight before it could progress. Trixie and Cocoa had run to get Gerald, because within seconds he was on the scene.

"What the fuck is going on in here? I'm running a business!"

"Your bitch took my bag!"

"I didn't do shit! And this bitch punched me in the face!"

"Lying bitch!" I tried to swing again, but the customer pushed me back.

"Give her the bag, Heaven. Or, pack your shit and leave."

Heaven's top lip twitched as she gave Gerald a look that could've killed him. "I don't have the bag."

"Siren, come with me," he said, pulling my arm back to where the lockers were. He grabbed the lock cutter and cut the lock to everybody's locker and just as I suspected, my bag was pushed inside Heaven's locker. I wanted to punch her again. Instead, I took the rest of the night off to calm my nerves. I knew the bullshit had only just begun. Gerald was not going to fire one of his top money-makers.

"Leaving already?" The Post Office Stalker asked as I treaded through the club.

"I need to get out of here."

"I know a great place to hide."

"I'm not going home with you."

"I didn't ask you to."

"Will you just leave me alone?"

"Your bad mood doesn't turn me off."

I stopped in my tracks. "What do you want, guy?"

"Just a date."

"Tomorrow, seven o'clock. I'll meet you on the corner of Canal and Magazine."

"I'll be there." He smiled.

Eight

"I guess you better tell me your name before I get in this car with you."

"It's Vincent Ruston, but call me Vince."

I stepped into the expensive, all-white Mercedes Benz. "Where are we going?"

"I had a taste for red fish, so we're going to Houston's. You like fish?"

"Not really, but if that's all they have, I'll eat it. I'm not picky."

"They serve a variety of things. You can order whatever you want."

It didn't take us long to get to Houston's. It didn't look fancy on the outside, but inside the atmosphere was calming and upscale. There was a stage for live music, a beautiful fountain, and large booths under dim lighting.

The waitress we received was friendly and quick on her feet as she walked from table to table.

After looking over the menu, I decided to give New Orleans cuisine a try. I ordered Oyster St. Charles as an appetizer and jumbo lumped crab cakes as an entrée.

Vince ordered wine for us to have with our meal and we talked and stuffed our faces.

"Are you going to tell me where you're from now?" he asked.

"No. Where are you from?"

"New Orleans, born and raised. I've lived a few other places, but there has been no place like home."

"What do you do for a living? You're obviously rich."

"Rich? No." He laughed. "I'm comfortable and manage my money pretty well. I could be rich, but I've created one too many bills for myself."

"Okay, so, what do you do?"

"I'm a Transport engineering manager."

"And how old are you?"

"Forty-six."

"You do realize you're old enough to be my father?"

"You're as young as you feel."

"You may feel young, but you seem like a dirty old man to me."

"I like what I like. You aren't a child and you most certainly don't look like one. Has anyone ever told you how gorgeous you are?"

"All the time. It gets old."

"If I were a woman and I looked like you, I'd take full advantage."

"I guess."

He smiled. "It's so attractive that you aren't aware of how beautiful you are."

"How is that attractive?"

"Because it makes you humble and not stuck up like most beautiful women."

I was tired of talking about my looks. "So, Mr. Vince, why hasn't some young girl married you, since you're so rich and well-mannered?"

"I've been married four times already. I don't think I can stand another. Those were the bills I was telling you about. I'll be free soon, though. I have a few more alimony payments."

I laughed and shook my head. "Nobody falls in love that many times."

"I do. There is no limit on how many people you can love or be in love with. You just have to grant yourself the proper healing when it all ends. Once you feel free, you can open yourself repeatedly.

"Wise too, huh?"

"I've picked up a few things here and there." He laughed. "Now will you please tell me something about yourself?"

"All right. Since we're talking about love and stuff, I've never been in a relationship."

"Really? Never?" he raised a brow.

"Nope."

"Why not? If I may ask."

"I've been focused on other things."

"It's shocking that some young man has never tried to make you his girlfriend."

"I never said nobody has ever tried."

"Basically, you specialize in rejecting men."

"If that's the way you want to look at it."

"My daughter is the same age as you and she's has more male friends than I care to mention."

"Oh, you have a daughter?"

"Yes. She's the same age as you."

"Does she know you like women her age?"

"She knows." He laughed. "Doesn't like it, but what can she do? I have to have a life, too. I'm still a man. I was that before I was a daddy."

"True," I said.

The server cleared our table and we lingered a little longer just talking. I still didn't tell him much about me outside of basics, like my favorite color: yellow, my shoes size: seven-and-a-half and my favorite soda: coke.

He dropped me back off at the corner where he scooped me up and teased me for not telling him where I was staying. I wasn't ashamed of living out of hotels, but I felt it was on a need-to-know basis, and he didn't need to know. I said my goodbyes, gave him my cell phone number, and headed up to my room to get ready to dance at the club.

I wasn't in the mood for Heaven or her bullshit.

55

Gerald grabbed me as soon as I walked into the club and escorted me to his office. He pushed me down in a chair. "Don't ever let what happened last night, happen again in my club. If you and Heaven have beef, squash that shit away from here. Do you understand?"

"Yeah, I got you," I said unmoved by his wrath.

"Good, you can leave."

I huffed and exited. I walked back out to the bar and took a seat.

"What's up, Siren?" Ferrin the bartender asked.

"Same bullshit, different night."

She shook her head. "I heard about what happened last night. Heaven does the most."

"Yeah, she does, but she's messing with the right one."

"You know why she fucks with you, right?" she poured me a shot of Patron.

"Clearly, she's jealous."

"Hell, wouldn't you be jealous if your man was checking out the new girl."

"Gerald? I don't want his dusty ass." I tossed my shot back and slid my glass for another one.

"That doesn't matter. You know some women are blinded by the dick."

"Glad I've never been that bitch and never will be." I rolled my eyes.

"I heard her telling Cocoa that she overheard Gerald telling you he wanted you or some shit."

"She's a damn lie. He came at me last night and she was in a private room. One of her pets must have heard and told her. Had they stayed for the whole conversation, they would have heard him get rejected."

Ferrin shook her head. "You better watch yourself around here. Nothing but snakes."

"I knew that the second I walked in."

I tossed back my other shot then headed to get dressed. Like usual, when I stepped in the room, everybody fell silent. I still hadn't spotted Heaven, but I knew she'd show her face soon. She was always in my grill. Her shadows, Cocoa and Trixie, were nowhere to be found either. Those bitches were up to no good.

I realized that I'd spoken too soon as Cocoa walked into the dressing room and rolled her eyes at me. I smiled at her and pointed my middle finger. She called me a bitch under her breath, and I let it slide since she wasn't woman enough to say it louder or to my face.

I finished up my makeup and changed clothes, so I could work the pole and make my money for the night. Cocoa took the place of Heaven, watching me as I danced around the club all night. Trixie eventually joined her and every now and then, they whispered. Ferrin kept the shots coming and told me that Trixie and Cocoa were scoping me because I'd given Heaven a black eye. I was happy to know I got a good lick in. I bet she wouldn't touch my shit again.

I packed up and headed out of the club at around three in the morning. Cocoa sat at the bar. I blew her a kiss as I passed her since she was admiring me. I saw her get up, but I kept on walking.

I needed to stop at Walgreens and grab a few things before I headed to my room, so I took a back street to the Walgreens on Chartes. The street was empty and the only light was provided from parking garages.

I felt a blow to the back of my head. I fell to my knees and got hit again. Kicks and punches came from every direction and even with my attempt to fight back, I could not block enough of the hits.

"You blacked my eye, bitch! I'll fucking kill you!" I heard Heaven scream.

"Bitch ain't so bad now," Cocoa chimed in as they punched and kicked me repeatedly.

"Hold that bitch down," Heaven instructed and that let me know Trixie was there too. I could feel the blood leaking from my lip.

Heaven snatched my hair.

Snip, Snip, Snip

She tossed the hair she cut from my head on top of me. "You're in New Orleans now, bitch. You need to go back to where you came from!" she spat then kicked me one last time and left me on the ground.

I rolled over on my side and groaned from the pain. She wasn't even woman enough to fight me one-on-one. A tear fell from my eyes as I looked at my hair now on the concrete.

"Oh my God!" I heard a car door slam and a woman rushed over to me, to help me from the ground. She helped me to her car and rushed me to the hospital.

The doctors ran tests and x-rays and discovered that I had two fractured ribs, a busted nose and lip, cuts on my arms and neck, a black eye, and a large, purple-ish contusion on the side of my face—possibly from a shoe, according to the doctor.

The beef was far from over.

Nine

My cell phone rang off the hook and I ignored every call. Gerald left several messages because he heard about what happened, but yet and still, Heaven and her flunkies still had jobs. He wanted us to have a sit down and smooth everything out. There was nothing to be discussed. He should have known that when I chose not to file a police report. I'd handle it on my own.

My room phone rang as I flipped through channels.

"Hello?"

"You are one difficult woman to get in touch with."

"Who is this?"

"Vincent."

"You really are a stalker. How did you get this number?"

"Common sense and luck. There aren't any apartments in close enough range from where I dropped you and you're new in town. I figured you'd be in a hotel somewhere."

"And you just so happened to call the Sheraton."

"It's the closest hotel to your job. I had a list. I just called that one first and what do you know, they had a Siren listed."

"Well, you found me. What do you want?"

"To check on you. I haven't seen you at the club this week and I've heard some nasty things."

"Like?"

"They said you got attacked."

"Did they say by who?"

"No, I didn't get that much information. So, how are you?"

"Healing. I have fractured ribs, so I can't dance."

"You should let me take care of you while you're not working."

Usually, I would decline his offer, but I did need a change of scenery. It was driving me crazy being in that room so close to the club and not being able to do what I wanted.

"How fast can you get here?"

"I'm already in the downtown area. I'll be at our corner."

"Cool, give me a minute to throw something on."

I tightened the wrap around my torso and dressed. I grabbed a fitted cap and tossed it over my hair. I couldn't do anything with it from that bad haircut Heaven had given me. My shit would never grow properly again, unless I shaved it all off. Even then, it would take years for the length I had to come back.

I grabbed my room key and headed down to meet up with Vince.

"Bruised and still beautiful," he said and I took a seat.

I pulled my cap down closer to my eyes and reclined my seat to take some of the pressure off of my ribs.

"So, who did this to you?" he asked and pulled from the curb.

"Three of the girls at the club."

"They must really be jealous of you? I hope you filed a report."

"No need."

"Why not? They need to be locked up."

"Nah, I don't want them in jail."

"You have a better heart than me."

If only he knew, this had nothing to do with having a heart. I had something.

It was called vengeance.

We drove for what felt like forever or maybe it seemed that way because I had no idea where I was. We crossed over a bridge of water then another long bridge after driving up a street named General DeGaulle.

"Where are we?" I asked, marveling at the big beautiful houses surrounding me.

"English Turn."

"I'm trying get on this level."

"You'll get here one day. Maybe sooner than later." He called himself throwing hints that I didn't care to catch.

His cell phone rang as we pulled up into his curved driveway. He answered, saying a few frustrated *okays* then hung up cussing.

"I have a bunch of worthless idiots working with me. I'm going to have to bail on you. Would you mind staying at my home for a few hours while I go handle something at the plant?"

"I'm already here, so I'll find something to get into."

"Help yourself to anything. I'll be back as quickly as I can," he said, pulling his door key from his ring. He was too trusting. "Think you can take care of yourself while I'm gone?"

"I'll manage," I said and hopped out of the car and headed inside his house.

It was obvious that women frequented his place often by the way it was decorated. There wasn't a heterosexual man on earth that would pick pale lavenders and pinks to paint a wall. I hoped he had a room in that house somewhere just for him.

Everything in his home looked expensive from the area rugs over hardwood and marble floors to the obviously custom-made furniture. His initials were carved into the back of the wooden chairs in his dining room. "Put a C in the middle and it'll say VCR," I said aloud to myself and laughed. *I'm so childish and lame.*

"Who are you?" a woman's voice scared me and I turned around.

"Siren."

"Siren from where?"

"I know Vince."

The woman rolled her eyes. "Great, another one."

"Another what?"

"Let me guess, you're between twenty to twenty-five, right?

"Twenty-one."

She shook her head, "Well, at least you're pretty and you're black."

"I think you have the wrong idea."

"You're dating my dad, right?"

"He's dating me, but I'm definitely not dating him. So, you're his daughter?" I said looking her up and down.

"The one and only. Is he here?"

"You're dad? Oh, no, he had to go back to the plant or something."

"Figures. He's either working or at that damn strip club. Now, what did you mean about you not dating him. Are you using my dad?"

"Not at all. I'm just not interested in him the way he thinks. I'm not into older men. I'm not into anything."

She laughed. "I think I like you. I'm Payton." She extended her hand.

Payton, like her dad, was tall, and she had beautiful chocolate skin with perfect white teeth.

64

He clearly only went for attractive women, because she was beautiful and didn't have a single feature of his. Her nose was slender and her mouth pouty like a Victoria Secret model.

"What happened to your face?" she asked. She was clearly a straightforward person.

"Long story." I looked down at the floor, insecure about my face now.

"It doesn't take away from your beauty." She smiled, noticing my discomfort. "Come upstairs, I'll show you around the house, since my dad is such a terrible host."

I laughed and followed her.

Vince had everything he needed in his house; everything except a strip club. He had a game room with pool tables, a movie theater, a workout room—everything.

"So, how'd you meet my dad?"

"I work at that strip club he's always at. Well, I used to work there. I'm not going back."

"Oh, you strip?"

"Yeah, is that a problem?"

"Not at all. I love strippers. It's just weird to know my dad does, too. Is Siren your stage name?"

"Yeah."

"What's your real name?"

"I don't tell anyone that."

"Fair enough. I won't push." She opened the last door in the house. "This is my room. Come in."

I followed her and walked over to her bed, not bothering to ask if I could lay on it.

She laughed. "Well, make yourself at home."

"Sorry, I just really needed to lie down."

"Something hurting you?"

"Yeah, fractured ribs."

"Ouch. I'm guessing that black eye was a lot worse than it is now."

"I was jumped."

"Oh, hell no." Payton swung around, showing a hint off hood. "I hope you kicked their asses."

"They got something coming."

Payton joined me on the bed. "I think I like you. Wait, I said that already, didn't I?" She giggled. "Anyways, since you don't like my father, you and I should be friends. I'd love company for the summer."

"You don't live here?"

"Oh, no, just in the summer and on holidays. I live in Atlanta. I attend Spelman."

"Oh, a good girl."

"Good? No. Smart? Yes," she laughed.

"I might have to take you up on your offer. It's not like I have shit to do. It could take anywhere from three to six months for my ribs to heal and I have to do all this stupid shit like practice breathing just to help the process.

"It's for the best. You need some aspirin or something."

"If you have any."

"I'll grab you some."

Vince didn't return until that night and I found myself taking to Payton; mostly by force since I couldn't leave. I didn't even really know where the hell I was. Payton sort of/kind of had the same aura as Kitty and for that reason alone I didn't mind her talking my ear of. I could possibly have a new friend. Time would tell.

T en

My ribs were still healing, but the scars, marks, and scratches had faded, and I only had one thing on my mind. I'd have to go against the doctor's orders to minimize my activities, because summer was almost over and Payton would be leaving for school. For two-and-a-half months, night after night, Payton and I watched Cocoa, Trixie, and Heaven leave the club to go home after their shifts. Payton wasn't the snobbish, rich girl people would peg her to be because of the way she carried herself. She was wild, crazy, and down for just about anything. She stood off to the side as I cornered both Trixie and Cocoa on separate nights and beat the snot out of them. I wore a black mask since she decided to record it and put it on YouTube. We named it Stripper Gone Wild. Tonight was Heaven's night. I had a special ass whipping on my heart for her.

"There she goes," Payton said as slowed the car down and watched Heaven leave the club. Just like every night since I beat the crap out of her fan club, a bouncer was escorting her to her car.

"What do you want to do?" Payton asked.

"Follow that bitch home."

Payton smiled and waited for Heaven to pull off. I watched every turn she made with my jaws clenched and my fist balled. Even with all the pain, all I could think about was that bitch cutting my hair. I wore large sweat pants and a black t-shirt. Tonight I wouldn't wear a mask. I stuffed the three things that I carried for the occasion in my pockets.

Heaven pulled into an apartment complex and parked a few cars down. I hurried and hopped out, ducking behind cars and moving towards Heaven, so she couldn't get too far. She was still in her car when I duck-walked behind it like they trained Marines to do. I pulled the little bottle of pepper spray from my pocket and positioned it to spray. I was ready.

"Heaven," I called out to her. She stood up and as soon as she did, I sprayed her directly in her eyes. "Thought this shit was over, bitch! Shoulda brought the guard home with you!" I yelled and she slumped against her car screaming with burning eyes. "Unlike you, I'm not going to beat you while your blind."

I walked over to her and grabbed her hair, snatching her head back. I pulled the bottled water from my pocket and opened it with my teeth as Payton stood looking for police and laughing.

"Move your hands!" I screamed. She didn't comply so I slammed her hands with her head on the roof of her car. Her hands moved just then and I drowned her eyes with the water then backed up.

"Fight me like a woman," I said and she dried her eyes with her shirt.

I held my fist up in front of my face, waiting, and in minutes, she charged at me like a raging bull seeing red. She swung and missed and I caught her face with my left. She stumbled. I gave her a minute to shake herself back then I tagged her ass again. It was no wonder she had to jump me. The bitch couldn't fight to save her life, and I didn't feel an inch of guilt for the ass whipping I was laying on her. She ran at me—chin up—and my fist crashed into her nose, making her fall back on the ground. Game over. I sat on top of her, pinning her shoulders down with my knees and pulled out the wireless clippers I had in my pocket with brand new Duracell batteries. She tried to fight me off, but was too weak. I shaved her head military style. I cut through the track, needle, and thread, punched her one more time, and left her right on the ground the same way she did me.

Payton and I ran to the car to get the hell out of sight.

We fell on the bed laughing in Payton's room.

"You messed that girl up."

"She had it coming. If you know you can't fight, you shouldn't start them."

"Remind me to stay on your good side, because I can't fight to save my life."

"After what you did for me, you never will. I'll beat up anybody you want me to." My ribs were sorer now, but beating Heaven until she was blue made it well worth it. I hissed and sat up in the bed.

"You okay?"

"Just hurting a little. I think that bitch caught me in the side."

"I'll get some ice."

Payton stood to leave the room and retuned quickly with ice wrapped in a hand rag. She sat down next to me. "Lift your shirt."

The bedroom door swung open and Vince stepped in. "How come I bring you here and you spend more time with my daughter?"

"Dad, don't be jealous. You should be happy I'm getting along with someone you brought home."

"I'm ecstatic, gives me hope. I just figured after all this time she'd be tired of you and want to be around me again." He winked at me and I cringed on the inside. He was still trying mercilessly to make something happen with us. "I'll see y'all later. I'm about to leave for D.C."

"You're driving seventeen hours?" Payton asked.

"Yeah, I haven't taken a drive in awhile. I'll see you two when I get back and try not to get into trouble."

"We're adults. Bye, Dad." Payton rolled her eyes.

"Bye, Vince," I chimed.

He gave us a nod then closed the door as he left.

"I hate when he talks to me like a child," she said and pressed the iced against my ribs."

"You'll always be a child in his eyes. You should consider yourself lucky. I never had parents."

Payton looked into my eyes. "That's the first time you've told me anything about your life."

"Yeah, well, not much in my life to talk about and be proud of."

"Tell me something else."

"I don't know what to say." I looked away.

"Okay, I'll tell you something about myself."

"I know everything about you. You never shut up," I teased.

"Forget you. I bet you don't know I like girls."

"What? You're not gay."

"Yes I am."

"What about all the boyfriends your dad has asked about?"

"All gay men."

"Get the fuck out of here."

"Swear."

"Why won't you just tell him?"

"That man would do everything but kill me. I don't want to see him disappointed."

"So you're going to lie forever?"

"Probably. Can I confess something?" she asked with shy eyes.

"Go ahead."

"I thought you were gay when I first saw you."

"What? Why?"

"Girl, you have stud written all over you. I don't care how tight your jeans are or what poles you've slid down, you have a boyish swag."

"You are not allowed to say swag."

"Leave me alone, but seriously, you do. You would be a sexy ass stud. Don't get me wrong, you rock the hell out of the femme look, but I can just see you in some boxers and a sports bra, sagging jeans, a cute haircut. You'd soak some panties.

I didn't know whether to blush or feel uncomfortable. "I bet the men who have had you got big egos."

"I have a confession now."

"What?" she asked anxiously.

"I've never had sex."

Payton snatched the ice pack from my side and stood up. "What!"

"Calm down, girl. It's not that big of a deal."

"Bullshit it's not. Its 2010, virgins don't exist anymore. Hell, I'm not even a virgin," she said, sitting back down on the bed. "We have to get you some sex."

"I've managed this long without it."

"You don't know what you're missing."

"Sweating and pumping doesn't sound that enticing."

"Then try women."

"And what the hell would I do?"

Payton tossed the towel on the floor like it didn't have ice it. She pulled her legs into the bed and moved to position herself between mine.

"What are you doing?" My heart began beating quickly.

"Shut up and trust me. Have I not proved myself worthy?" she asked as she tugged at my sweat pants.

"Payton," I protested. "Tell me what you're doing."

"About to give you the sensation of sex. You don't have to be penetrated to get the feelings."

"Are you—"

"Do I ever beat around the bush with you, Siren? I'm about to eat your pussy. Unless you have reservations, I suggest you relax." She tossed my pants to the floor. "Damn, it's all pretty and perfectly intact." She ran her fingers across my pussy and I jumped. "No one has even touched you down here?"

I couldn't find my words, so I shook my head.

"Moan as loud as you want to. I hate quiet studs."

"I'm not a stu—" My words were cut off by the swipe of her tongue.

Payton licked slowly and I could feel every tongue stroke. She placed my hand on her head when she realized I had no idea what to do with them. I pulled her sheet from the bed and my toes curled as her head moved up and down. I thought about the movements of her tongue with my eyes closed: up and down, side to side, *shit…* circles.

What the fuck is she doing to me? She leaned up to take a breath. "Fuck my mouth," she said as she pushed my thighs up and down against her face until I did it on my own. *Ooh's and Aah's* escaped me along with some *mmm's* and cuss words.

"S-t-t-t-oooo-p!" I moaned as my legs tensed from the tingling that rose up from my toes. I couldn't take what was happening. It was too intense. I tried pushing her head away, but she had a death grip on my thighs. There was literally an explosion between my legs as my clit pulsated on its own. I was breathless and lay with my hands over my eyes. "What was that?"

"You just experienced your first orgasm."

I could hear her smile through her words, but I refused to face her.

Eleven

Siren,

I stared at your letter for weeks. I'm sorry that it took me so long to respond, but I had to find my words. I am a broken man right now, and I feel like I don't have another reason to live in this world. The only peace that I've found in this situation, in all this time, is that someone might have possibly loved her the way that I did. She told me about you in a letter when she first met you. She said a few other things about you, but I'm not sure I can disclose her secrets. That's how we were, ya know. I kept her secrets and she kept mine, even the ones we were ashamed of. Now I don't have anyone to talk to. And please forgive me if you feel that I've been a bit rude for not at least saying thank you for what you are doing for me by keeping money on my books. I'm not your responsibility and yet you chose to take it without being asked. Thank you,

Siren. Thank you. I'll keep this short and sweet, but know that you are truly appreciated.

Corey

I found myself sitting at dinner tables with Vince, thinking about Payton as he wined and dined me. I had no idea what she had done to me, but whatever it was that she made me feel, I was addicted to it. I pretended to be interested in Vince just to continue being trusted in his home. He tried me for sex a few times, but my body rejected him before my mouth did.

Each time that he took a flight out, Payton's face was between my legs. The more we sexed, the more I needed it from her, and laying on my back for her just wasn't cutting it anymore.

"Tell Payton I'll call her in the morning," Vince said as he dropped me off in front of his house and pulled off for another trip.

I headed inside with the key that he always trusted me with and saw Payton standing in their large kitchen—stainless steel kitchen—hovered over the clearest glass of water I'd ever seen in my life.

"Deep in thought?"

She jumped. "I didn't hear you come in. I was in another world. Deep in thought as you said."

"About what?"

"Tonight's my last night here. Then, it's back to Georgia for me."

"I'll miss you," I said leaning on the island in the center of the kitchen. Her backside faced me.

I stared at her slender frame as she bent over. Something in me changed as I thought of how sexy her body was. I'd been around plenty of naked women, but there I was, feeling an attraction I'd never felt before. I wanted to touch her and not in a friendly way. I decided to let go and let my body do what felt natural. My feet moved toward her and before she could swing around, my pelvis was pressed against her backside.

"Mmm, what's this?"

I gripped her waist gently. "I'm not sure, but go with it," I answered and ran my hands up her sides and pulled her to stand straight up. I planted a kiss on the back of her neck. "Let's go to your room," I whispered.

"Finally acting like the stud I see in you, huh?"

"I don't know what I'm doing. I just want to touch you."

"Touch away," she said seductively and eased herself from between the counter and me.

I followed her, flipping off the light in the kitchen.

In the bedroom, we stood face to face in darkness.

"Kiss me," she requested. "We never kiss."

"I've never kissed anyone before."

"You truly are a virgin, well, slightly." She giggled. "Try me." She placed her hand on my face and pulled me toward her, pushing my lips apart with her tongue the same way she had been doing my pussy.

Her tongue felt warm as it slid against mine and her head moved from side to side every now and then. She pulled back. "What do you want to do to me?"

"Whatever will please you. Teach me," I said then reached to pull my shirt from my body.

Payton taught me what she liked done to her body, showing me her most sensitive places. I only had to be told once. After that, it was a wrap. I started at her neck, running my tongue along the veins, then tracing her collarbone. The way her body reacted turned me on. Her chest rose and soft breaths released from her lips as though I had the softest touch on Earth. Her eyes closed and her head turned slowly, opening a new place on her neck for me to sensationalize.

"Take off my clothes," she whispered and I did as she wanted, taking mine off, too.

I remounted her after I undressed and pulled one of her roused nipples into my mouth. Eyes closed, she grabbed the back of my head, and her chest heaved upwards once more. I squeezed the flesh of them between my fingers, not knowing I could love a person's body so much. I was going all the way tonight.

"That feels so good," she moaned.

I pulled my lips away and licked my way to her panty line. For the first time, I was face to face with a pussy. Like me, she was shaved and the skin was smooth. I caressed it, admiring it.

"It's now or never, Siren," she said.

It was now, right now. I licked it once to see what it tasted like and instantly I was hooked. *Just do what she did to you.* I dove in, wrapped my mouth around her lady and went to work, swiveling my tongue in every direction. *Damn, she tastes good. This is what I've been missing. I wonder if she's really moaning from what I'm doing or if she just trying to make me feel good.*

"Siren," she said breathless. "You lied to me. You've done this before."

She's not faking it. I pulled her clit into my mouth, sucking it gently.

"I want you inside of me," she demanded, pulling my face from her pink passage.

I moved up to meet her puckered lips and slipped a finger into her like I'd been doing it all my life. I moaned as I entered her wet and warm cave.

"More," she whispered as I finger-stroked her and fell in love with the flesh inside of her.

I eased in another finger and the moan she released vibrated through my entire body. Pleasuring her was pleasing me. Her reactions boosted my ego and my hand moved faster inside of her. Her wailing was a cry for more of me and I gave her what she wanted, what she needed. Her body began trembling and her walls squeezed around my fingers.

"I'm… I'm cumming," she struggled; biting down on her bottom lip to hold back what I knew was coursing through her body. She shook and shivered while I kissed all over her face.

"How did I do?" I asked once she released and relaxed.

"Girl…"

"What?"

"You were born to do this," she teased and turned over to wrap her arms around me. I looked down at her arm, tensing up a little bit.

"Cuddle with me. Talk to me."

I didn't want to do it. After it was all over, I didn't want to touch her anymore, but I didn't want to make her unhappy or upset so I did what she asked.

"That felt so good," she whispered and kissed my chin. "What are you thinking about?"

"I can't believe I had sex with a girl."

"You never get used to it either. I still find myself thinking about the fact that I'm really gay. I'd marry a girl."

I laughed. "I don't know about all that. I've never thought about marriage."

"Maybe I'll be able to change your mind." She snuggled closer and dozed off to sleep.

I lay with my eyes wide open, thinking about how Kitty would be teasing me right now, because I ragged on her so badly about being crazy about women. Now there I lay, ready and wanting to jump back into the warm box.

T welve

A cool chill ran over my body as the covers were snatched. "What the fuck is going on in here?!" Vince yelled.

"Shit!" I jumped up from the bed and Payton hit the floor. We both scrambled for our clothing. Vince ran for me first and caught me by my throat.

"Whore!" he screamed in my face. "That's my fucking daughter!"

"Daddy!" Payton screamed and ran to try and pry his fingers from around my neck. He knocked her to the floor.

"I wine and fucking dine you and all this time, you're fucking my daughter!"

"Daddy!" Payton cried. "Don't hurt her, please! It was me… it was all me. I came on to her. I'm gay!" she screamed.

Vince slammed me to the floor and turned to face Payton. "You're what?!"

She held her hands up to block him if decided to hit her. "I'm gay," she whined.

"Get the fuck out of my house! Both of you!" he screamed and stomped out of the room. Vince was no longer Mr. Nice Guy in a suit.

Payton crawled over to me and I sat up holding my side.

"I have to stop getting into fights or my ribs will never heal," I joked to ease the mood and the tears that started falling from Payton's face. She stood and helped me from the floor.

"Get dressed. We're going to your room until he calms down. I don't want to go back to Georgia with him angry."

She was quiet. We didn't say anything else. We left Vince's house and went to my hotel room. I stared out of the window the entire ride *across the river*. It was time for me to make a move. I'd been in New Orleans too long and I was involved in a lot of bullshit.

"Are you angry with me?" Payton asked.

"I'm good."

"You haven't said a word to me since we left."

"What am I supposed to say?"

"Something. Anything."

"I said it's cool. I knew you had to go back to your life eventually."

She sighed. "What if I asked you to come back with me? Would you consider it?"

My mood instantly shifted back to a good one. "Come with you? Are you serious?"

"Yeah, I think we'd have fun together. I don't want us to end like this, so come with me."

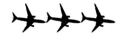

Corey,

I was so happy to see that you'd written me back. I'd hoped that I didn't make you uncomfortable. I still miss Kitty every day and I think about her constantly. I think about both of you. She always wanted you to be okay, so please don't thank me. You are my brother now, even if I am not your sister. And don't feel that you have no one to talk to now. I'm willing to listen whenever you are ready to talk. As I stated before, I never stay in one play too long. I've actually overstayed my welcome here in New Orleans and in the morning, I will be on my way to Atlanta, Georgia. Shit has been crazy. I have all this beef with these three strippers that I used to work with. I got caught up sleeping with the daughter of a man who was pursuing me. I'm still shocked that I'm sleeping with anybody's daughter. I'm sorry if I've said too much or shocked you in anyway. I used to tell Kitty this stuff. I told her everything and I'm still upset that she was taken away. Anyways, I'll do just as I did here and set up a P.O. Box and mail you the address when I get there. I don't know what's in store for me in Atlanta, but I guess I'll see.

"What are you doing?" Payton asked, walking out of the shower, her hair wet and a towel wrapped around her body.

"Writing a letter."

"To who?"

I didn't like her questioning me. "My brother."

"I didn't know you had a brother."

I didn't offer her a response.

"Where is he?"

"Could you stop with all the questions?" I said, licking the envelope and sealing it shut.

"I'm sorry, *yeesh*." She rolled her eyes and plopped down on the bed. "You all packed up?"

"Yeah, I don't have much. I just need to stop at the post office before we go."

T hirteen

Atlanta, Georgia

"You're a terrible traveling partner."

"Huh?" I said, adjusting in my seat.

"You slept the whole seven hours. I thought I was talking to you and you were knocked out."

"Sorry," I laughed. "I don't know what it is about cars and planes. They just make me sleepy."

"I'm glad I decided to drive during the day because I'd be screwed depending on you at night."

"Get off my back. Are we stopping to eat soon?" I stretched out my arms.

"What do you have a taste for?"

I gave her a naughty grin.

"Besides that."

"Something good. I don't care."

"Something good to me may not be good to you, so what do you want?"

"Chicken."

"Oooh, you'll love chicken and waffles."

I turned up my nose. "That sounds disgusting. Waffles, syrup, and chicken? Pass."

Payton laughed. "Don't knock it until you try it."

"What else you got?"

"Do you *have* to have chicken?"

"No, but something fast would be nice."

"All right, I'll take you to one of my favorite places to eat. Steak n' Shake."

"Mmm, a chocolate shake sounds damn good right about now."

Georgia was starting out with five stars already as I bit down into my Portabella Swiss burger. My mouth watered with every bite. Payton watched me, laughing as I moaned with each bit like I had never eaten a burger in my life. I wanted to kiss whoever discovered that combination of things between bread, fresh bread at that. And don't even get me started on that shake. I was ready for another nap after that. I wiped my mouth with my napkin.

"Girl, you still eating? Dang, you eat slow."

"First off, I like to savor my food and not devour it like some homeless man who won't get another meal for days. Hey, you brought me here. You knew these burgers were good. You should have waited a few days to bring me here."

"I'm just getting started." She winked. "So, I was thinking. How would you feel about going to a gay club with me tonight?"

"A gay club? They have those?"

"Honey, there is a club for everything."

"I've never been to a club outside of stripping."

"You really do only care about making money. I'm surprised you haven't lost your mind being out of work all this time."

"Don't think it hasn't crossed my mind. I'd much rather be looking for a club to dance in tonight over just standing in one."

"You'll have time for that. You're here with me and I got you. Don't worry about anything."

"I don't want you to have me. I can take care of myself."

Payton shook her head. "Do you not know how to just enjoy life? You do not turn down a woman that just offered to cater to you."

"That catering is going to be limited from the look your dad shot us when we pulled off from his front door this morning."

"He just needs time. He might not speak to me, but he'll keep the cash rolling into my account. He does not want to deal with my mother."

"Does your mom know that you like girls?"

"Yeah, she's known for years. She knew before I did."

"How is that possible?"

"I guess she saw something that I didn't."

"Now that you and I have… you know… does that mean I'm gay, too?"

"I think you are, but that's ultimately up to you to decide. Would you like to try men?"

"Honestly, I've never had an attraction to men. I've always just wanted their money. I could say a dude was cute, but never did I ever think to have sex with one or anyone for that matter."

"It still shocks me that you're a virgin."

"Hey, the way we do it works for me just fine. I love the feelings."

Payton smiled. "Maybe I'll teach you a bit more when you're ready, but in the meantime we need to get to a mall, because you're going to the club with me. I'm not taking no for an answer. Oh, and I'm dressing you."

"I can't pick my own clothes either?"

Payton laughed and stuffed the last of her veggie wrap into her mouth.

Lennox Mall was next on the agenda.

While shopping, Payton had plenty to say about what she thought my style was and the type of stud she saw me as. I was clearly only in the mall to make sure whatever she picked up fit, because she made all the selections and swiped her black card to pay.

I had to admit that I did feel good in the boy clothes. As soon as I put on the baggy attire, my stance shifted; I felt relaxed and swag was added to my walk. Payton licked and bit her lips at me. I looked good. I was a stud, almost.

'Rude Boy' by Rihanna blared through the club, but was quickly shut off as the DJ announced that if there was a fight, the club was getting shut down, and the ten dollars we paid was non-refundable. The song picked back up where it left off and Payton asked if I wanted a drink. She then dragged me through the club by my hand toward the bar. Girls smiled and winked as I passed them and I smiled back. One chick even grabbed my hand just to let me know she was watching.

I tugged at the collar of my shirt and bobbed my head to the music. I stopped in front of a mirror in the club and stared at myself. I had no idea I could look so good in men's clothing. Payton had been throwing the word *stud* around since I met her. I finally decided to let her dress me like one since she swore up and down that was the way I acted. She put me in a plaid, short sleeved, Polo shirt, Levi jeans, and red and white Polo shoes and of course, she accessorized the whole fit with a red Atlanta hat. Hats had become my new best friend since I still hadn't figured out what to do with my hair after the bad haircut. I just moisturized it daily and pulled it to a ponytail at the bottom of my neck. That was all it was long enough to do.

Payton handed me the drink she got for me and pulled me close to the stage.

"Why are we standing over here?"

"So we can see the shows."

"Shows?"

"You'll see," she said and sipped her drink.

I glued my eyes to the stage when the announcement of the start came through the speakers. Everyone pushed against each other to watch. The first performer was announced and when a man dressed as a women came out to the stage, my mouth dropped. He moved his lips perfectly to Melanie Fiona's 'It Kills Me' and his formfitting, navy blue, sequin dress sparkled. Women and men held up dollars as he stood in one place singing dramatically. I couldn't take my eyes off him.

Payton nudged me and smiled. He was working for those dollars, hell he even made me dig into my pockets. He got fifty dollars from me easily. Who knew lip-syncing could be so powerful?

"Oooooooh, I gotta be out my mind, to think it's gonna work this tiiiimeee. A part of me wants to leave, but the other half still believeeeeesss..."

I wanted to apologize for whatever it was that I did and beg him to take me back. He bent over and touched my face and I damn near passed out. I stood blushing and Payton was eating it all up. She laughed herself to tears.

The song ended and they announced the next performer. The girls in the club went crazy. 'Neighbor's Know My Name' by Trey Songz started to play before anyone stepped out. While everyone screamed and hollered, I was simply anxious. If the next performer was anything like the last, all my cash would be on the stage floor.

The curtain finally swung back and a short stud stepped out, dancing seductively and playing to the crowd, well the feminine women. I was in a daze as

91

she moved, pulling her clothes from her body, and rolling her stomach. She hopped down off the stage and sat on the edge, pulling a girl's face to her lap to make it look as though she was sucking her off. She threw her head back with her mouth opened for added effect then flipped back onto the stage rolling on her head. The money flew as she danced from one end to the other, mouthing the words here and there. She spun around and paused and the lights and music dropped. They flipped back on, and Chris Brown's 'No Bullshit' bellowed. Even I wanted to jump up and down a little bit. That was my shit. I awed at the way she moved her body and not because I wanted to get with her. I began daydreaming that it was me standing on that stage, enticing every woman in the club while they threw money at me. It could be me.

Fourteen

"Are you comfortable?" Payton asked, naked beneath the covers and with her chin propped up on her hand.

"What are you asking me?"

"Are you comfortable being in my apartment. I'm not trying to pry or anything, but I noticed that you never talk about a home, your parents… you were living in a hotel."

"I'm comfortable," was the only response I offered. People always said they weren't trying to pry, but that's exactly what they did.

Payton changed the subject. "What got into you last night?"

"What?"

"Excuse my French, but you fucked the shit out of me. What was on your mind?"

I smiled. "I was just excited after seeing that girl on stage."

Payton frowned. "What girl? There were plenty."

"The one that danced to Trey Songz."

"Oohhhh. Liked what you saw?" She smirked.

"Not like that... she made me miss dancing. I've never seen anything like that before. Strip clubs were cool, but now that I know I can dance for women and make just as much... I need to get into that."

"You want to be a stud stripper?" she asked in a questioning tone.

"Hell, why not?"

"I didn't mean to sound discouraging. I think you'd be good at it, although I've never seen you dance."

"Girl, I got moves."

"Ass clapping isn't exactly moves. Although, it could work in your favor." She giggled.

"Whatever."

Payton tossed the covers back on the bed and hopped out, walking around the room naked. She grabbed a laptop bag and ran back over to the bed.

"It's freezing in here," she said and sat the bag over her lap to set it up. "Let me show you something."

It only took a minute or two for her laptop to power on. I watched as she logged onto the internet and typed YouTube into the URL.

"You really love that website, don't you?"

"It's entertaining," she said and typed in *stud strippers*.

"What are you doing?"

"If you're thinking about doing this, you need to see who you would be competing with. This is King Kellz, one of my favorites," she said, biting her lip.

We sat watching her top four favorite stud strippers; each of them having something special about them: Juicebox was a master of stunts; Face commanded the room with her looks alone, Pretty P had no limits, and King Kellz could really dance her ass off—professional choreography style. The motherfuckers had me wanting to toss dollars at their asses. The glistening look in Payton's eyes and the comments below the videos confirmed that dancing in gay clubs was what I wanted to do. She closed her laptop and looked over at me.

"You still sure you want to do this?"

"Positive."

"Like *sure,* sure?"

"What? You think I can't do it?"

"I don't know."

"Put some music on."

Payton reopened her laptop and picked a song at random. R. Kelly's 'Number One' began to play and she sat the laptop to the side. I eased from my side of her bed and snatched the cover. I walked over to her, grabbed her ankles, and slid her to the edge of the bed. She blushed and tried to look away but I turned her face back towards me and lip-synced the song while looking into her eyes and rolling my waist in front of her. I ran over to her dresser and grabbed the red, Atlanta fitted cap she bought for me and pulled it down over my frizzy ponytail. I walked back over to her, straddling her legs and rubbing my pussy against her thighs.

By the time the song was over, Payton and I were getting it in on the floor.

"I wasn't expecting that," Payton said, sipping orange juice. She sat a plate filled with eggs and bacon in front of me.

"Told you I had skills. What now? How do I get into dancing for clubs?"

"Sign up to do a show. I can handle that part for you, but first we need to get your look together. I really think you have the best of both worlds since you danced in gentlemen's clubs first. You can pull off a femme and a stud look."

"I feel that."

"Are you attached to your name?"

"Siren? Not really."

"Good, because now that you'll be dressing more like a stud. You need a name that fits." Payton looked up to the ceiling, thinking.

"Toxic," she said aloud. "Nah, that still sounds too feminine. What about Notorious?"

"Like Biggie Smalls? Uh-uh, more original."

Payton stood and walked over to the fridge. "I need more juice," she said, opening the door. She gasped. "I got it!" She pulled out a blue and white can. "Cream!"

"Cream?"

"Yeah and what's the first thing you think of when you hear that word?"

"WuTang Clan."

Payton laughed. "No, silly, but that's still perfect for you. I'm talking about seduction, making girls cream." She smiled.

"I like it." I smiled back while rapping CREAM in my head. *Cash rules everything around me, C.R.E.A.M get the money, dollar, dollar bills y'alllllll.*

After my approval, Payton went for her cell phone and started making calls. I listened while she set up appointments for my hair, face, and body. It was like being under the eye of Ms. Weston all over again, only this time, with my permission.

In a few hours, after driving all over the city of Atlanta from one shop to another, Siren died and Cream had taken her place. They started with my hair first. Had my hair been at its full length, I would have cried when the stylist turned on her clippers and shaved the sides of my head. She took scissors and cut off any permed hair that I had left and shaved the back and edged me up. I bucked my eyes when I looked in the mirror. I had always known I was beautiful, but seeing that much of my face with my hair cut all the way around with a mini fro in the middle, made me lust after myself the way the other people did. I wished Kitty could see me.

Payton and I spent the rest of the day talking about the gay community. She told me the good, the bad, and the ugly. We discussed labels and how gender roles were becoming a big thing in the lesbian community, because studs were beginning to be treated like men. She told me I'd get criticized because I didn't mind girl clothes and makeup; some people wouldn't view me as a "real stud". Payton had it down to a science. By time she was done explaining every label, I was dizzy, but into it. I'd crossed over and there was no going back.

Fifteen

It was do or die time. Nothing in life had ever had me nervous or second-guessing myself, because I never had the chance to think. Wait... I take that back, because this lifestyle and fucking Payton for the first time made me nervous. But usually, I dived into everything head first and eyes closed, hoping whatever I got myself into worked in my favor. This, tonight, I had to prepare for. Payton gave me pointers on how to play to the crowd. She let me know that this was not a gentleman's club where men came to toss money if they had it. These girls would make me work. And my moves better be worth them passing on buying a drink. I scanned the crowd from behind the curtain.

I looked down at the outfit that Payton dressed me in. It was both masculine and feminine: a white mid-drift halter and baggy shorts. Payton really played into the androgynous idea, coloring my eyelids with yellow and my lips with a soft pink. I was ready to perform.

My heart dropped when the song ended. I knew I was next. I listened for the announcer.

"All right y'all, we have a special treat for you tonight! This is her first night performing so show her some love. Coming to the stage… *Cream!*"

"Break bank," Payton said and I turned and smiled. She winked and left to join the crowd.

I eased out to the stage, nervously. My heart pulsed loudly and drowned the screams of the anxious women. I wasn't as confident as I was when I danced. For me, men were easy; any little thing made their dick stand upright. Women were critics and would stare at you if you were lame as hell.

The music kicked on and I jumped into character. I was Usher, performing 'There Goes my baby.' The women around the club lifted their hands in the air and snapped to the beat while grinding their hips.

Move your feet.

I walked to the side of the stage and sang to a girl sitting on the edge. She was the first to hold up a dollar.

Touch her.

I kneeled down beside her and grabbed her chin and she blushed.

Quit being a pussy… perform.

I had to turn it up a notch. I had everybody's eyes and I wanted to keep them. First impressions were lasting impressions and I needed to leave a great one in order to get booked again. I jumped down off the stage and walked through the crowd looking for a victim, and then I spotted a pretty petite girl hiding behind her friends. Payton told me to go for the shy ones. Ms. Pretty Petite covered her face as I reached for her and pulled her in close to me. I tuned everybody else out as I made invisible love to her, kissing her neck and invisibly stroking her in sex positions. When I was done, I was covered in money. I smirked and danced my way back to stage, collecting dollars and shedding the little bit of clothing that I did have on. Studs started to tip too.

There was a miniature celebration inside my body as I stepped off that stage and ended my first performance. Payton collected my money from the floor while I gave myself invisible high fives. I was satisfied and couldn't wait to feel that rush again. Girls still screamed even after I was gone and that, to me, was confirmation of a job well done.

"Maaaan, shawty, that was off the chain," a feminine voice said from behind me. I swung around to see the stud from the week before.

"Thanks."

"How long have you been dancing?" she asked.

"Like this? Tonight would be the first."

"I don't believe that. You killed it though. Maybe one day we can hook up and do a show together."

"Maybe." I nodded and she held out her hand for a dap and left to prepare for her performance.

I smiled and Payton rushed to the back and hugged my neck. "You did so good!"

"You think so?"

"Hell yes, those girls are still *creaming* as we speak," she teased. "I think I'm a little hot and bothered myself."

"I just might have to handle that for you."

"You sure will, but let's count this money first. I have to get my fifteen percent."

"Fifteen percent?"

"Yes, for booking the show and getting you ready. Consider me your manager."

"Wait, hol'up. I never asked you to do any of that."

"How else was it going to get done? Look, chill out, I'll take my fifteen tonight and you can handle yourself from now on, if that's what you want."

I sighed. "No, it's cool. I'm just tripping. Thanks for everything," I said and headed to change into regular clothing. I had a flashback of Ms. Weston getting over on me. I had to shake the bad taste she left in my mouth. I needed Payton until I could figure all this shit out on my own.

Payton dropped her keys on the coffee table, rustling her fingers through her hair as she headed for her bedroom. I went into the kitchen to grab a bottle of water.

"I got you something," she said, walking into the kitchen with a black, plastic bag in her hand.

"Why do you keep buying me stuff?"

"I just like to and I think this gift could be beneficial for both of us."

"What is it?"

"Open it," she said, a seductive look in her eyes.

I rummaged through the bag and pulled out its contents. "It's a fake dick."

"It's called a strap and I want you to use it on me."

"And how is this beneficial for me?" I grinned.

"Practice for your show. Might add to the fantasy if you wear it sometimes when you perform."

"Uh huh. And when did you want me to use this on you?"

"Now," she said and pulled her shirt over her head, tossing it to the tiled floor. Next went her bra and the shorts she wore to the club. "Put it on."

"I don't know how."

Payton grabbed the strap from my hands. "Get undressed," she demanded and I followed. "You are so fuckin' sexy," she said, piecing the strap together and pulling up my legs to secure it against my body. She hopped up on the counter and spread her legs. "Put it in. Feel around if you have to."

"I won't have to feel around," I said, walking up to her and teasing her crease with the artificial penis. "You want this?" I asked, taunting her.

103

"Yes, give it to me. Show me you can move just as good in this pussy as you did on that stage tonight.

"You don't want me to taste it first?"

"No, I... Oooooooh," she moaned as I shocked her, filling her with eight inches. "Shit," she groaned and I pushed in deeper.

I moaned, too, as I squeezed inside of her slowly. I didn't think there was another thing that could top the feeling I got from the first time I received head. This was a completely new level of sensation as I mimicked manly strokes. The back of the toy rubbed my clit with each stab. I felt a sense of power and control as I held onto Payton's legs and decided how she would get the dick.

"Faster," she begged through gruff moans and bulky breathing. She held onto my neck and kept her eyes closed as I danced inside of her. "Fuck me, Cream."

Hearing my new name sent me into overdrive and I began pounding her. She wailed now, digging her nails into my shoulder and biting her bottom lip. I wasn't a man, but I felt like *the man* as she announced her pleasure. *"I'm about to cum"* was the sexiest shit I'd ever heard in life. Just hearing her say it made me cum.

"Fuck!" I cussed, waiting for her to join me.

Five more long strokes and I enticed her into the same place as me. She squealed with tears running down her face and sweat across her brow. Exhausted, she said, "You are the truth."

If the clothes that Payton bought for me didn't change me, strapping her most definitely did. I felt confident and powerful knowing that it was me that controlled her sexual titillation. I lay smiling. She had created a monster.

Sixteen

"Sometimes, I lay here, and I think about how different my life could have been if my mama wouldn't have left us, and my daddy wouldn't have done what he did. My family was dealt a bad hand," Kitty said, pushing the pillow under her head as we lay face to face.

"At least you know where you come from. I don't know anything about my parents. I don't even know why they gave me up."

"I wish I didn't know. Having no daddy at all is better than having one that touched you."

"I guess you're right."

"Whoever your parents were, they missed out," Kitty simpered. "They could have gotten to know an amazing person. I knew we'd be friends the day that you walked into the club."

"How'd you know that?"

"I have a gift. I can read people."

"You sound crazy."

"It's true. I really can."

"All right, read me right now. What am I giving off?"

Kitty was silent, staring at me with her piercing eyes. "Emptiness. You're hollow inside."

"That's not true."

"It's very true. I can feel it. You've been empty since I met you."

"I got plenty on the inside."

"You got nothing. I watch you dance every night and you don't even seem to enjoy it at all. I know why I am where I am and why I do what I do. Do you?"

"I do it for the money."

"That's all?"

"What other reason do I have? What other reason do I even need?"

"You have to have a goal."

"Nope, I just want to make money."

"I feel sorry for you, Siren. You're going to spend the rest of your life existing instead of living."

"I'm breathing, so I'm living."

"You know what I mean."

"Are we about to talk about love again?"

"What's wrong with love? One day—"

"It's going to hit me. I know. I know. You'll have a reason to love then and you won't be able to run from yourself. Whatever that means…"

"You're such a bitch," Kitty teased.

"Yeah, yeah. Goodnight, Kitty," I said.

I turned over in the bed opening one eye and flinching from the stare of Payton.

"Who's Kitty?" she asked, not letting me take a second to compose myself.

"Someone from my past. Wait, how do you know about her?"

"You justsaid her name in your sleep."

I laughed. Payton was the first person I'd ever shared a bed with. It was funny to hear someone tell me about a sleeping habit that I had.

"So, who is she?" she pressed.

"Why?"

"Because its not the first time you've said her name. I just never said anything before."

"Why are you choosing to say something now?"

"Because she has to mean a lot to you if you're saying her name all the time."

Her tone and demeanor put me on the defense. She sat with her arms folded across her chest and much attitude in her voice.

"It's not your business who she is or isn't," I replied, not used to being questioned.

"You don't have to get defensive. It was just a question."

"One that I don't want to answer."

"All right, I'm off it," she said, swinging her legs from the bed and standing. "I'm going to make us some breakfast. Oh, and you've been booked for another show."

"Cool, thanks," I said, turning over.

She and I had a discussion about her managing me since I spazzed on her when she asked for fifteen percent. I had to realize there was no difference in paying her the way I paid the owners of the strip clubs I danced in.

I slept in for a few more hours, not bothering to join Payton for breakfast. I'd been caught up in her world for so long that I forgot that I had things to tend to. I hadn't even written Corey to let him know where I was. Today would be the perfect day to do that since Kitty weighed so heavily on my brain.

I sat in the middle of the bed, updating Corey on everything that was going on in my life. I didn't know what the hell I was thinking, moving to Georgia and changing the way I lived. I trusted Payton too much and I knew it was because she had introduced me to this new lifestyle; introduced me to who I had to have been all my life. I had to be disconnected from *me* for a reason. *Right?*

The newness of the feeling pulled me in like nothing ever before. I just wanted to be on stage again.

Girls screamed my name with dollars in their hands for giving, for funding. Music shook the walls of the club, while some studs stared with jealous eyes from the corners and others respected the hustle and held their dollars out, too. I was a natural born performer. I mouthed lyrics and rolled my oiled body beneath the neon lights.

The first performance had been the ice breaker but that night, I was more confident than ever while I searched the crowd for a victim. Payton would be starting school soon, so she decided to record the performance for YouTube, because she didn't know when she'd be able to film again. She didn't want to waste anytime when it came to promoting me.

Once my show was over, I headed to the back to change. I needed a drink. Payton rushed over to me, her eyes and mouth wide with excitement.

"What are you so happy about?"

She lifted her phone and held it close to my face, but I couldn't make out the words.

"Back up. I can't read that."

"You've been requested to dance in Maryland."

"Huh? How? I'm still making a name for myself here."

"Yeah, I know. My mom actually lives in Silver Springs and so do most of my friends. I was telling one of my friends about you and she pulled some strings to get you booked at a gay club out there in Baltimore. Travel and hotel all paid for."

"You're pretty good at this management thing." I smiled.

"I know right, makes me feel like I picked the right major. It also helped that I told her you were my girlfriend." She hurried and spoke as I opened my mouth to debate the girlfriend part. "This is great practice for when I'm ready to work with celebrities. I'm so excited!" She hugged me.

I'd later regret not correcting her right then. "When is the show?" I asked.

"Next weekend. I won't be able to go with you since school is starting, but I'll handle all the business aspects of it."

"Cool. I can't wait. Nothing I love more than getting on a plane."

"You're going to love it there," she boasted. "Get dressed. You deserve a drink. I'm going to make you a star in the gay community."

Se(x)venteen

Baltimore, Maryland

"So, you're Cream?" A beautiful peanut butter colored woman asked with a naughty grin on her face.

"The one and only," I said, matching her flirtatious tone and stopping in front of her as she stood near baggage claim.

"I'm Ana. I requested you." she offered her hand.

"Well, it's much appreciated since I'm still trying to make a name for myself."

"Looking like that, it won't be a problem." She licked her lips and I knew it was only to show me her tongue ring.

"Shall we go?" I said, motioning toward the exit. I let her step away first.

"You travel light," she said, looking at my duffle bag dangling from my shoulder.

"I don't require much. I'm easy."

She laughed. "I'll make a mental note of that."

I couldn't take my eyes off of Ana's swaying hips and ass bouncing. I didn't know what was happening. The gay thing was still fairly new to me since Payton was the only woman I had crossed that intimate line with, but I was lusting over Ana in the worst way. I heard East Coast women were beautiful, but my God. I wanted her to keep talking to me with that strong Baltimore accent, putting extra emphasis on her O's and U's.

Ana led me to her car, and we drove to the hotel I'd be staying at. She handed me cash to eat with, winked at me, and sent me on my way. She told me she'd be back at nine to pick me up for the show. I was ready.

Ana spared no expense on my room. I walked into a lovely suite with everything that I could possibly need. It was like a miniature apartment. I'd never even purchased rooms that nice for myself. I only needed the room to sleep. I sat my bag on the floor and my phone rang. Payton didn't give me a second to unwind.

"Hello," I said.

"I know you've landed. Why didn't you call and say you made it."

"I was with Ana. I didn't want to be rude."

"I don't think she would have minded a two-minute phone call."

"Well, I'm here. I'm going to rest and shower, if that's okay with you."

"Why the attitude?"

"Look, I'm tired. Can I just hit you later?"

"Yeah, sure. Break bank and have fun," Payton said, hanging up in my face.

I shrugged my shoulders and fell across the bed. I needed food, sleep, and a shower.

"Tonight's going to be a goodnight. Everybody say, yeah!"

"Yeah!" the crowed barely roared.

"Hold the fuck up. What was that weak bullshit? I'm going to ask this one more time and I want you all to wake the fuck up. It's going to be a good night. Every say, YEAH!"

"YEAH!" everybody roared.

"We got a special treat for you tonight all the way from Atlanta, Georgia. She is sexy as shit. We need to show her how we do it in B-More. Give it up for Ceam!" the VJ yelled and the music started to play.

There was no stage in this club, so I walked through a door and stepped out onto the floor. The crowd stood in a circle with the middle of the floor cleared. Eyes drilled into me lustfully and before I could even move, the money started to fly. The women on the East Coast were not shy as they approached me, stuffing cash into my jeans. I took my position to do my thing and a woman approached me from the left with money clenched between her teeth. When she got close enough, I snatched her, pulling her close since she dared to be so bold. I grabbed her legs and in one swift movement her legs were wrapped around me. Her friends, along with everyone else, cheered. I took a woman approaching me during a show as a challenge. She'd back down before I did.

She rubbed her hands up and down my arms as I bounced her against my pelvis. I eased her to the floor on her back and moved down to give the illusion that I was going to eat her pussy. Why the hell did I do that? I was in for the shock of my life when the horrific scent of her unclean pussy jolted into my noise. *Oh, hell, the fuck no!* I jumped up from the floor and left her lying right where she was and quickly entertained the first woman I saw. She knew she was wrong for that. She should have stopped me from even going down there.

I lured a few more women into my tricks, even turned out a few studs. One stud in particular kept her eyes on me. I figured I danced on a chick she was feeling by the way she mugged me and clenched her jaw. I kept on doping what I was doing until the music stooped. I collected my money and headed to the back.

"You are something else." A sweet voice said. I turned to see Ana leaned against the wall.

"Where have you been hiding?"

"I never hide," she said, walking closer. "When you're done getting dressed, meet me at the bar," she winked and walked away.

I dressed quickly; ready to be in her presence. The shows were still going on as I headed back out to the loud music and dancing. Girls grabbed my hand while I walked. My ass was pinched, and studs dapped me off. Ana flirted with the bartender and when I approached, she turned her flirting towards me.

"What do you drink?" she yelled over the music.

"Patron, mostly."

She ordered a few shots and moved close, pressing her breast against mine. She wore an all-black, sheer cat suit and her red heels put her at eye level with me.

"Would it be too forward if I asked you to come home with me?"

I bit down on my bottom lip. "What about my room? It's already paid for."

"It's my money. Come home with me." She enticed me with her made up eyes.

"It's not good to mix business with pleasure."

"Then give me back the money for the room and flight," she teased. "I'd rather be pleasured."

"I get the feeling you always get what you want."

"Trust that feeling."

I looked from the corner of my eye and the same stud that mugged me as I danced, mugged me now. She held a drink in her hand and her fitted cap was pulled down low against black shades that she wore.

"You know her?" I nodded in her direction.

"Magic? Yeah, I know her."

"She's been staring at me all night like I pissed in her drink or something."

"Magic always looks like that. She's a professional boxer. They are all angry, if you ask me. I don't know what her clown ass doing here anyways. She can take her ass back to Silver Spring. All that money and she shacking with her motha." She turned up her lip and I smiled at her B-more accent.

"Bad history there?"

"Something like that. Anyways, forget her. Are we leaving or what?"

"Lead the way," I said, not protesting this time. I was in a new city with a banging broad willing to kiss the ground I walked on. I was not about to pass up on seeing what her insides felt like.

Ana had been on mind since she dropped me off at the hotel. I liked Payton, but I didn't want her to be the only woman that I ever experienced anything with. It would be damn near impossible to resist all the beautiful women that surrounded me: big ones, small ones, tall ones, short ones, dark ones, and light ones. How could anyone just choose one?

I wondered about Kitty. She was hell bent on falling in love. I wished she could see me now. I was hell bent on falling in lust as I followed Ana's ass out of the club.

"So, what type of girls do you go for, Cream?" Ana asked.

"I'm not really sure."

"No type?"

"Not really or I just haven't discovered it yet."

"You think I'm attractive?"

"I think you could have anyone you want."

She laughed. "I think the same of you. You have a girlfriend back home?"

"Home?"

"Yes, where you live," she said sarcastically.

"Oh, no."

"Even better," she said and we hopped into her car. She keyed the engine and floored her way home. We rode with the windows down and the music loud. Every few seconds she reached over and touched me, licking her lips and smiling. I couldn't wait to see her naked.

Once we pulled into her apartment complex, she threw the gears into park and leaned over, pulling my neck to her mouth to suck on the flesh. She tugged gently and flicks of her tongue teased me. I closed my eyes and let her do her thing.

We headed inside and didn't waste any time. Ana stripped at the door and I did the same, lifting her up like she was a member of my audience and carrying her over to the sofa. She reached her hand between our bodies, pressing her fingers to my clit, almost making me drop her.

"Am I allowed to touch you?" she whispered.

"You already are. Should I be protesting?" I asked, laying her down her on back and running my tongue across her collarbone.

"Mmmm," she moaned, curling beneath me. "Let's see if you fuck as good as you dance."

"Let's see if you taste as good as you look."

I loved my life. I was going to fuck Ana until it was time for me to board my plane.

Payton was sitting on the sofa when I entered her apartment with the spare key she'd given me. It was early, so I expected her to still be asleep. It was the reason I didn't call her to scoop me from the airport.

"Hey," I said and sat my bag down near the door.

"Hey? I called you all night. Why didn't you pick up?"

"I stayed at the club late, then I went home and crashed so I wouldn't miss my flight."

She sneered. "Is that right?"

"Yeah, that's right."

"I heard a different story."

"From who? I wasn't with anybody."

"So, you didn't leave the club with Ana directly after the show?"

I took a step back. "Who told you that."

Payton jumped up from the sofa. "I told you I had friends out there. How could you fucking disrespect me like that?!" she screamed.

"How did I disrepect you?"

"Psh, Magic saw you all up in Ana's grill. She called me as soon as you two left!"

"Magic?" I said, recalling the name when Ana told it to me in the club. No wonder the bitch was looking at me crazy.

"You have people watching me now?"

"Don't flip this. Nobody was wathcing you. She goes out all the time and this time she just so happened to see you disrespecting me. Do you know how I felt when she called to me how my *girl* was acting?!"

"Whoa! Pause. What do you mean your *girl*?"

"As in girlfriend." She rolled her neck and all of her Spelman education went out of the window.

"Girlfriend? When the fuck did I become your girlfriend? I let that little comment slide the one time you said it since it got me a show. How did it become the truth?"

"We might not be in a relationship, but when you move into somebody's home *for free*, eat their food, spend their money, and fuck them. They deserve some respect!"

"When did we have a conversation about even being exclusive?"

"Why did we need to have it, Cream? You're sexing me."

I took a deep breath to calm myself. I had to think about what could happen here if it escalated further. Payton was my manager and my ride around the city since I refused to buy a car. I had to keep the peace. I still needed her.

"You're right. I shouldn't have left with Ana. It was disrespectful. Would you please calm down?"

She folded her arms across her chest. "Did you sleep with her? And be honest. You've told enough lies today."

I took a deep breath and rolled my eyes. "Yes."

"Wow," she said, throwing her hands up. She dropped her arms to her side and shook her head. "I need to go for a drive." She turned to walk away and returned with her keys. She brushed past me, huffing and stomping.

"Payton," I called out, but she ignored me, grabbing her purse and leaving.

I didn't know what to do. Technically, I was single, but I still felt like I'd done something wrong. I didn't ask for all of this. It just happened and I was just being myself.

The front door slammed and Payton walked in. She tossed her keys into her purse and tossed her purse on the sofa. I sat in her dinning area at the table.

"How was your drive?" I asked.

"Nice," she said, opening the fridge for a bottled water.

I tapped my hand against the table. "I guess you're still mad at me."

"You guessed right."

"I don't understand what I did wrong."

"Of course you don't. You wouldn't."

"What is that supposed to mean?"

"Nothing, Cream," she said, leaning against the counter.

I sighed. "I'm sorry you felt disrespected."

"Cream, just stop it. Don't apologize. You don't even know what you're apologizing for. I don't know why I'm expecting anything more from you."

"More?"

"Yeah, I thought we were trying to create something together, but on my drive, I realized that's not happening at all. I don't even know your real name."

"Payton—"

"Unless you're going to tell me something about yourself, I suggest you just don't even say anything to me." She pushed herself from the counter. "I need to study. We can just carry on like we've been carrying on." She headed toward her bedroom. "Oh, you have a show booked in Florida next weekend. Try not to fuck the client this time. I don't manage prostitutes," she said and went to her bedroom and slammed the door.

I sat staring at the floor.

Eighteen

Miami, Florida

Gabriella bounced her ass against me on all fours as she moaned and gripped the sheets. I slammed into her, full on. My puma throbbed beneath the harness of the strap as she took every inch with no issue.

I really did try my best to comply with Payton's request not to fuck the client, but after laying eyes on the Black and Mexican beauty, I couldn't resist. The good thing this time was that Payton didn't have any friends in Florida. Nobody surveillanced me when I left to blow out this pretty chica's back. I did tell myself that I wouldn't eat at her buffet and I kept that promise to myself.

Gabriella didn't seem to mind that I didn't put my mouth on her. She pushed me inside of her wetness and pulled my strap into her mouth to suck off her own juices. My mouth dropped. I couldn't feel a damn thing, but it was some sexy shit to watch as her pretty pink lips moved back and forth. I wished just for a second that it was real. *Damn.*

Gabriella lifted the harness and began giving me head without bothering to even remove it. I was still leaned up on my knees and I was about to fall over as she worked her tongue against me like she'd been eating box all her life. *Holy shit!* She was better at it than Payton.

"You taste so good," she took a breath to say then dove right back in, twirling her head to imitate the motions of her tongue.

"Cum for me, Papi. Cum in my mouth," she moaned.

Did she just call me Papi? Chicks do that? Hmm, kind of sexy… I think.

I grabbed her silky hair and pushed her closer to apply more pressure against my clit. I was going to give her what she wanted. She hummed as she licked and I grinded against her tongue for added sensation. A few more thrust forward and it was all over. I collapsed on her bed and she laughed, wiping her mouth.

"Cream, Cream, Cream," she said, smiling. "You don't play with that strap. No one has ever made me cum that fast before."

"You're fucking with the wrong people," I teased, still out of breath. "You are the truth with that mouth."

She truly was and comparing Gabriella to Payton, made Payton seem mediocre.

"I do what I can." She licked her lips. "When can I expect you back to Florida?" she asked.

"Whenever you book me again."

"Don't tell me that. I'll book you twice a week," she joked.

"Hey, money for me, pleasure for you." I shrugged my shoulder.

"We better get some rest, so I can get you to the airport on time."

I sat up to remove my strap and she grabbed my shoulder. "Leave it on. I like to feel it against me as I sleep." She smiled.

I didn't have a problem with that.

I didn't get a second to breath. Payton rushed at me on the first level of the airport. She snatched my duffel bag from my shoulder and I immediately saw red as she unzipped it and dumped everything inside on the floor.

"What the fuck is wrong with you?!" I yelled and everyone around us stopped to watch the drama unfold.

Payton picked my strap up from the floor and shook it in my face. "This! I bought you this and you take it with you to fuck another bitch!"

I snatched it from her hands. "You really have to do this in public?"

I walked around her, ignoring the tantrum she was throwing, to pick up everything she dumped out. She was lucky I didn't believe in causing scenes because I would have knocked her on her ass for touching my bag. I put it over my shoulder and a crowd started to form just that quickly. I walked away.

"I'm talking to you!" she yelled and I kept on going. She pushed me from behind and I dropped my bag.

"Bitch!" I screamed and charged at her, grabbing her by her neck. I exhausted everything, trying not to hit her. "I'm not your fucking girlfriend! You were the one who told me to wear the strap for shows. Now you're checking me in public and shit? You better get your ass to this car before we both get locked up!"

My reaction shocked Payton. Her eyes bucked and she inhaled as I released her neck and picked my bag up once again. She ran past me, through the automatic sliding door, to her car parked right out front and hopped in, speeding off without me.

I threw my hands up and then sat them on my head, locking my fingers and took a deep breath. She was really trying me. I walked over to the cab stand and paid for a taxi to take me to her apartment. I had a show that night and wasn't in the mood for her *girlfriend* attitude.

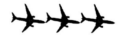

"You're not going to say anything to me?" Payton asked as I packed for my show.

"Say what? You left me at the airport. We're done talking."

"You fucked another bitch with the strap I bought you."

I pulled the strap from my bag and tossed it at her, hitting her in the face by accident. She gasped.

"Did you really have to do that?"

I shrugged. "Did you really have to cause a scene in the middle of the airport?"

"You hurt me, Cream. I reacted."

"Yeah, like a child."

Nineteen

HoustAtlantaVegas

If Payton thought I was out of hand before, she hadn't heard anything yet. The bookings started coming in like crazy after my shows in Maryland and Florida. I was the next YouTube sensation in the community when my Baltimore show went viral. I wasn't even sure who recorded it, but I appreciated it. Payton showed me the performance and I patted my self on the back for a job well done.

Before long, girls were paying for private dances and just like the rappers and athletes, I had groupies lining up. Some I *knocked down* and others I didn't.

My name made it all the way to the Chi (Chicago). In only a few months, I'd visited Miami twice, making sure to make a pitstop between Gabriella's legs; Las Vegas—and believe that what happened there definitely stayed—New York, New York, definitely a city worth being named twice. Hell, three times would work for me. They show major love and the women were downright gorgeous. Los Angeles cashed out on me and for the first time, I had my chance with a sexy snow bunny that was a dancer, a flexible one. But out of all the cities that I visited, I loved Houston the most. The girls in the crowd weren't shy at all when I pulled them from their friends. They challenged me, imaginarily having sex with me on the dance floor.

The best part about all of it was that I didn't pay for a single thing. They booked my rooms, my transportation, and they fed me. I was on top of the world.

Ana booked me for a second show on the East Coast. I was shocked that Payton had even told me about it since she damn near had a meltdown the last time I'd gone and messed around with Ana.

Ana waited for me at the airport like she did the last time, a Kool-Aid smile spread across my face involuntarily as a reaction of our previous memories.

"Hey, you." She smiled.

"Hey, beautiful," I said, wrapping my arms around her then following her to her car.

"Was your flight okay?"

"First class is always good for me."

"Glad to hear it."

"I'm surprised I'm even here. Payton flipped the last time."

She snickered. "I figured. I put two and two together when my emails went unanswered.

Remember that chick Magic that was staring at you in the club that night?"

"Yeah."

"That's Payton's best friend. It should have dawned on me then, but I had my thoughts elsewhere." She bit her lip and her eyes perused my body. "I booked you using a different email and name." She smirked.

Ana took me back to her place where she fed me a home cooked meal, sexed me real good, and helped me prepare for my show.

The club was way more packed than it was the last time I was there. Ana gave me a wink and sent me on my way. She made her rounds in the club, hugging and kissing studs and gay men. I scanned the crowd for Magic, but I didn't see her. I knew she had to be in there somewhere, if Payton had anything to do with it.

I made it my business to pinpoint Ana as my victim for the night just because I knew Magic would be lurking somewhere. Payton wasn't my chick and I was going to confirm that.

When my show started, Ana stood conversing with a group of studs. I walked up slowly behind her and bent her over. She looked back and smiled as I danced against her ass and bit my bottom lip like I was really digging inside of her. Dollars fluttered over my head from the stud standing in front of her completely amused by my display. I yanked Ana up by her hair and she looked over to her left. Her expression changed soI looked, too.

There was Magic.

I grinned and swung Ana around, pulling her legs up around my waist and carrying her to the middle of the floor. The spotlight followed. She grinded against me and I sucked on her neck. Everybody in the place was rattled, screaming, and throwing dollars. By the time I was done bending Ana into a pretzel and licking every nook and cranny of her body, everybody was sweating. I was sure that some hardcore sexing went down that night.

Ana helped me to collect my money then followed me backstage.

"What was all that?"

"Just had to prove a point to your girl, Magic."

She laughed. "You used me? I'm cool with that."

"I know it." I smiled. "Payton's not my girl and she needs to stop acting like it."

"I feel that."

"I'll meet you out front."

Just as Ana turned to head to the front, Magic appeared, pushing her back. "What the fuck, Magic?"

"You better stop disrespecting me!"

"Nobody's disrespecting you. We're not together anymore!"

"What's the problem?" I stepped up behind Ana.

"Nobody's talking to you. Where'd you find this 'Bama ass bitch?"

"You don't know me to be calling me out of my name."

"I know you're foul. Ana, move so I can have a few words with your friend."

"Magic, cool it." Ana pushed her in the chest.

"True shit, you need to get out of my way."

"You doing too much," Ana scolded.

Magic pushed Ana out of the way and came straight at me. I didn't remember much after that. I remember swinging and missing. People came out of nowhere to break up the fight and the next thing I knew, I was in Ana's bed with ice on my eye. I'd never lost a fight in my life. I didn't feel too bad about it though since Magic was a professional at beating people up. I didn't go down without a fight, though. I was just happy it was only a black eye. I could cover that with makeup.

"I'm so sorry, Cream," Ana said, sitting beside me on the bed.

"What are you apologizing for?"

"Because this is my fault. I should have known Magic would be there, and I should have told you more about our history."

"It's not important. I seriously doubt she swung at me because of you. This had everything to do with Payton."

"You think so?"

"I know it. She could have said or did something the first time that I came if this was about you. She just needed an exuse to fight me."

"We can call the police and press charges. You know boxers aren't supposed to fight on the street. I'll be happy to bring that bitch down."

"Nah, that's too far. I'll deal with the root of the problem myself."

T wenty

"You just don't quit, do you?" I said gathering my things for another show.

"So it's my fault that you got your ass whipped?"

"Magic is your friend. You think she would have come at me for any other reason?"

"Okay, so, I'm wrong because my friend loves me and doesn't want to see me hurt?"

"Why do you keep finding your own messages in my words. It was fucked up. Point blank."

"No, what's fucked up is you making a fool of me, fucking all these girls like you're not coming here to lay your head. It's stupid and it's childish."

"I'm just doing me. There is no crime or childishness in that. You said yourself that you didn't expect anything more from me."

"You don't think that what you're doing is childish? And wreckless on top of that? What if you catch something from these random chicks? What happens if I catch it?"

"I haven't even been fucking you. I'm not bound to you, Payton. I'm not yours," I said, zipping up my bag and tossing it over my shoulder. "The only reason I stay here with you is because you've done so much for me, and I don't just want to bail on you and seem unappreciative. This isn't even me. You're walking around like you own me or some shit. I'm not yours for the second time. Did you get the message in that or do you need it spelled out?"

"Spell it out, because last I checked, we do everything that couples do."

"Okay, three times a charm. Im. Not. Your. Girlfriend." I clapped my hands together with each word. "We fuck and we go out to eat. Woopty-doo."

"Wow. That's how you feel?"

"That's what it is. Look, I have to go. I have a show."

"And how are you going to get there? I'm not bringing you, and you don't have a car."

"I got here when you left me at the airport that time, didn't I? Taxies are twenty-four seven." I pulled my cell phone from my pocket and dialed information for a cab company. I had no shame in being dropped off to the club in a taxi. My money was at the club. I would get it by any means necessary.

Me and my duffle headed outside to wait. I hoped a police officer or security guard wasn't driving around. I wasn't in the mood to get reprimanded for loitering or simply being black on a Saturday night. Get offended if you want, but racism and profiling was and is still alive and thriving.

The yellow taxi pulled up in fifteen minutes and I was gone. Payton called my cell back to back and each time I silenced the call. There was nothing she could say to me. I needed to do one of two things: get over my fear of having a car after my horrible incident with Kitty and buy one, or find another chick with a car that could navigate me through the hilly streets of Georgia.

"Twenty even," the cabby said and I paid him.

The line was wrapped around the club when I stepped out. Familiar faces winked and waved as I headed up to the front for my VIP entrance, and a few new faces smiled in my direction.

"What's up, Cream?" the stud bouncer out front greeted me.

"What's up?"

"No Payton tonight?"

"No, she's back in school and cutting down on the club scene. I'm on my own for awhile."

"Cool, cool. Well, go on in. The ladies are amped to see you perform tonight."

"I hope their amped with their purses."

"I hear that."

I patted the bouncer on her back and headed inside. Club owners were good at deceiving the crowd. There was maybe ten people inside and that included the bar tenders and security. I shook my head and headed over to the bar for a drink. As the bar tender poured me a shot, a group of women were allowed inside. They were loud and wore sashes across their shoulders, each a different shade of black. The tallest one wore the word "Bride" across her body. The back of her head faced me, but her body was enough to say she was as attractive as the curves that moved with her footsteps. She turned finally, laughing with her friends and I damn near fell. She was a shocking resemblence to Kitty: her fair skin, perfect smile, and tiny, pointed nose.

The pulsating of my heart knocked so loudly that my ears seemed to be thumping. This annonymous and strangely familiar beauty had rattled me. She moved closer and my heart sped up. More people entered the club, but my eyes were fixated on the Kitty dopple-ganger. Like an idiot, I pinched myself then turned to ask for another shot. I tossed it back once received and still the split image stood before me, closer now and hanging over the bar to order a drink.

"Make their next round on me." I said to the bartender, handing her more than enough money to pay for the women's drinks. It was only five of them. Three attractive and two not so much. I ordered one more shot then forced myself away from the bar.

I sat in the dressing room staring at myself in the mirror, and like always, Ms. Weston stood behind me, brushing my hair and telling me how beautiful I was. She would tell me her life and how she used her powers for evil, taking rich men for all that they had, but still had nothing to show for it. I should have known then that she didn't care about anybody but herself.

Her late husband, Barry's father, was twelve years her senior. She met him when she was twenty-one and he believed he was getting a young dummy. She milked him dry, took his house, his car, and everything in his bank account, which is why I didn't feel bad for having the deed to her house. She admitted to me proudly that she broke him down. Life was a game to her and she wanted to be the best player at it.

"Cream?"

I turned away from the mirror.

"You're on next, honey."

"All right," I said and pushed myself away from the vanity. It was time for me to get lost on the stage.

As usual, the girls screamed. Dollars began to fly before the music started. I was making a name for myself quickly, and I knew a lot of it had to do mostly with Payton's promotion skills. If I owed her credit for nothing else, I owed her that.

As I moved around the stage, my eyes searched the crowd for the look alike. Now was the perfect time to get up close and personal with her and not come off as some creeper. She and her friends still occupied the bar, so I needed to make my way back there. I had six minutes.

I jumped down from the stage and parted the crowd like the Red Sea. Girls reached for me, rubbing their hands down my back and stomach and sliding cash into my jeans. I enticed them the whole way down the aisle, but my main focus was Twin. Her friends giggled and blushed as I stopped eight feet away and pointed my finger at her while rolling my belly. She covered her face, flushed by my sensual movement directed toward her.

I moved closer when she didn't step down from the stool she sat on, bending down and gripping her ankles. She wore a short skirt but I didn't care. You must be prepared for these things walking into a gay club or any club where there are performers. Her friends screamed and I lifted her ankle to my shoulder and pretened to lick from where I touched to her inner thigh. Her hands remained over her face; the embarrassment evident in the way she shook her head side to side. This was my ice breaker because after the song was over, I'd be able to talk to her with ease. I had no real reason for wanting to know her, other than the fact that she reminded me so much of Kitty.

Her friends tried effortlessly to strip her hands from her eyes, but to no avail. Usually, I had limits to the things I did to women, but I needed to see her face. I leaned into her and licked my tongue across her fingers and voila, like magic, her hands were removed. She screamed then laughed and her friends did the same. She was focused on me the rest of the dance.

Once the song ended, I rushed to collect my dollars and head back behind the curtain to put on some regular clothes. Everybody knew that I never stayed after I did my show, so eyes followed me. I ran back out front without my duffle bag and searched for the look alike. She'd migrated to the other end of the bar. I proceeded with caution and one of her friends spun around with a wide grin on her face.

"I loved your show," she said over the music.

"Thanks. Who's the bride?" I asked, looking down at her sash that read "Bridesmaid". She turned and pointed to the look alike.

Duh, Cream. I was so busted staring into her face.

"Hey, you! Come over here!" Another one of her friends who stood closer to her yelled. The friend beside me looped her arm with mine and drug me over to the bride. I stopped directly in front of her.

"Thanks for the dance." She laughed.

140

"Anytime," I said, smiling at her Atlanta accent. She was clearly a native or lived here more than five years.

"I appreciate the drinks, too."

"The bartender snitched on me?"

"She sure did." She smiled, and I couldn't help but take the stretch across her lips as something contagious and joined hers with my own.

"We're going to dance!" Her friends yelled and they walked away to leave us alone.

"Aren't you going to go with them?" I asked.

"I'm not much of a dancer," she confessed.

I nodded my head, feeling awkward being left alone with her. I didn't know what to say. I figured I'd stick to the obvious. "Big day tomorrow?"

"Yeah."

"Nervous?"

"A little bit. It's such a permanent thing and I'm still so young, but it's what I wanted."

"How old are you?"

"Just turned twenty-one, so I'm celebrating double. Getting older and my last night of freedom."

"Happy belated birthday and congrats. Where is the lucky lady? Don't lesbians have joint parties?"

"You'd know better than me. I'm not gay." She laughed.

"Oh, shit. My bad."

"It's cool. You were right to assume. This place was my friend's idea. I wanted to do something different, rather than the male stripper thing."

"Hey, you two need to get on this dance floor. Take these shots!" Her friend popped up behind me, holding glasses between *Bride* and I. We took them and inhaled them quickly.

"What's your name?" I asked.

"Tasia. And yours?"

"Cream, everybody calls me Cream, on and off stage."

"Enough of that. Let's dance!" Her friend interuppted and pulled us both by the wrist and lugged us to the floor. As long as Tasia was there, I was going to be there.

Tasia and I danced circles around each other for a little while, and to say she wasn't a dancer she was pretty good at it. I respected her space and the fact that she was getting married by keeping my hands to myself. I violated her enough during my show. Being close to her was enough, because she possessed the same warming spirit as Kitty. Her friend kept the shots coming, but Kitty didn't drink all of hers. The ones that she declined, I took for her.

After the last, I began feeling dizzy, which I was surprised didn't happen sooner with the way I tossed back those shots.

"I think I need to sit down," I yelled to Tasia.

"Me too."

We both sat and I hoped to sober up, so I could call a cab. My head spun and Tasia and I leaned against each other. The music faded.

T wenty-one

A soft hand tapped me lightly on the shoulder, then the taps got harder and turned into shakes. "Cream get up. Cream… get up."

I groaned and rolled onto my back, struggling to open my eyes.

"A woman, Tasia?"

The sound of a male voice was the medicine for the hangover I knew would come. I sat up quickly, letting the covers fall to my waist without relizing I was shirtless.

"Fred, I swear this isn't what it looks like."

"I guess my mind is playing tricks on me. How could you? The night before our wedding."

"Fred." Tasia scrambled from the bed and I sat frozen. I thought any sudden movement would set him off. I was not in the mood for a replay of what happened with Payton's father.

"I hope it was worth it!" he spat in her direction and she ran toward him, begging and pleading to explain. "Get your hands off me!" He snatched away and she threw herself at his feet.

"Fred, I'm so sorry. I got drunk. I-I-I don't remember anything. I swear I wouldn't cheat on purpose."

"Do you even know what time it is?"

His question made me look over at the clock in the hotel room: *1:34p.m. Shit.*

"Fred, please!" she cried out.

"Stay away from me! You can come get your shit from out of my house! I hope this dike can take care of you!" He turned to exit the room. Tasia crawled after him, tears leaving a trail for her to find her way back to the spot where she lost her love and her potential marriage.

"Freeeeddd!" she sobbed and the door slammed, leaving her to deal with whatever it was she thought she'd done. Even I couldn't fill in the blanks for her.

I wasn't sure if I should stay or go. I sat in the bed and watched her on the floor, curled into the fetal position and saying her fiance's name repeatedly. She shifted a little, and getting a glimpse of her face, made me decide to stay. She looked like Kitty crouched on that floor and if she were Kitty, I'd console her.

I stepped from the bed and grabbed my shirt to at least cover the top half of my body. I then spotted my boxers and put those on, too. That made me half-way decent. I walked over to where Tasia lay, tiptoeing so as to not disturb her pain or make it worse with my presence—the evidence that what happened was reality. I touched her back lightly and she cringed, so I jerked away then tried again. This time she accepted the comfort that I offered. I helped her from the floor and walked her back over to the bed.

"You need me to do anything?"

She shook her head no.

"Okay," I said and went to search for the rest of my clothes.

"Wait, can you find my phone for me?" she asked.

Where the hell is my phone? My damn duffle bag? "Shit, I need to get back to the club," I said, now panicked and realizing I was going to have problems of my own when I walked through Payton's door.

"I'll take you," Tasia said then moved to get out of the bed as if she were forcing it.

"I can call a cab."

"No, I'll drop you wherever you need to go."

She searched for her phone and we were on our way. She drove slowly up and down the hilly street of Atlanta, dialing each friend from last night, but only getting an answer from one.

I didn't know if you could call what I was doing eavesdropping since we were in the car together, but I did strain my ears to try hearing what was being said on the end of the phone.

"Have you spoken to Lottie... I called her three times already and her phone keeps going to voicemail... Onya, I honestly can't tell you a thing that happened last night." Tears began falling down her cheeks. "He came into my hotel room last night," she sniffed. "I know... I love you too... Okay." She hung up.

I was afraid to say anything to her, since I was fifty percent of the reason that she was five and a half hours late for her own wedding. I couldn't imagine what she was going to have to deal with when faced with her family and his.

"Can I ask a question?" I went ahead and said.

"Yeah."

"Why were you staying in a hotel alone, anyway? Shouldn't your bridesmaids be in a room down the hall or something."

"It wasn't supposed to be a major thing. I was in a hotel because I live with my fiance. He and the boys stayed at his house and I got a room so we'd be separated the night before."

"Did anyone at least try to call you?"

"No."

"You don't find that odd?"

"Yeah, that's why I need Lottie to call me."

"Which one was Lottie?"

"The one buying the shots. The girl drinks like a damn fish, but will wake up the next day with a full memory like all she had was water the night before."

"I'm really sorry about all this."

"It's not all your fault. I should have kept my promise to myself not to drink. I have to fix my own mess," she sighed. "Do you remember anything from last night?"

I drew breath. "Let's see, uh, no… not really. I remember drinking and dancing."

"So there may be a slight chance nothing happened between us?"

"Yeah, slight."

"Would you be willing to say that to my fiance?" she said as though she still had one.

I nodded my head.

Tasia slammed on brakes and did a u-turn in the middle of the street. Her foot was now heavy on the gas and just like the Graviton Spaceship Ride at fairs, my back was pressed to the seat, and I couldn't move.

We pulled up to a nice, conventional one-story brick house.

"Come with me."

Tasia rapped on the door like the police. We knew someone was home, because there was a car in the driveway. She knocked again and this time we heard the latch being undone. The door creaked open, no "who is it" or nothing.

"Lottie?" Tasia asked with confusion in her face and voice. "What are you doing here? I've been calling you all morning."

"Fred called me. The man is a mess."

"You answered his calls and not mine?"

"He needed me."

"I needed you!"

"Baby, who are you talking to?" asked the same male voice that awakened me from my sleep.

"He sure sounds like he's a mess. What's going on here, Lottie?"

Her friend took a deep breath. "Look, I'm not going to beat around the bush with you. Fred and I are in love. He didn't want to marry you, but didn't want to hurt you."

"What are you saying to me?"

The door stretched open further and Fred appeared with an 'oh shit' expresson on his face. I turned my nose up at his Fresh Prince of Bellaire haircut. Was he serious?

"Fred go inside, I told you I'd handle this."

"Handle this? I'm not some situation that needs to be handled! I'm your best friend. His fiancee." Tasia said and backed away. "It all makes sense now. You set me up! Why would you do this to me!" she yelled and I backed up to make room for the confrontation that was about to go down. This was better than a three a.m. episode of Cheaters.

"Tasia, I never meant to hurt you," Lottie said, as if she was truly apologetic.

"Fred?" Tasia looked to him for some response, some explanation. He hung his head.

"Y'all deserve each other," she said and walked away.

That's it?

I followed Tasia to her car and my respect followed. Right then, I knew the type of woman she was and it wasn't the bust-your-windows, key-your-car-up kind.

She did, however, break down the moment she was in the car. Her face fell forward on her steering wheel and she sobbed. She leaned back and started the engine and I sat with no clue of what to say or do.

She cried as we rode to the club to retrieve my bag and she cried on her way to drop me home.

"Will you be okay?" I asked with one leg dangling from her car. She didn't say a word, just nodded then sped off once I closed her door. Now I had to deal with my own life.

"I called you all night last night and several times this morning. You care to explain where you were? I was worried sick!"

"Back up out of my face, Payton."

"And whose car was that? It sure didn't look anything similar to the taxi that picked you up last night."

"You're watching me now?"

"I have to. It's the only way I know anything. Why must you disrespect me, Cream?"

"Let me stop you. First off, I'm not your girl for you to check me. I could have sworn I made that clear last night. Secondly——"

"So you stayed out all night and half the day to emphasize a point?"

"Let me finish. You don't control me, Payton."

"This has nothing to do with me trying to control you. It's all about respect. I moved you here, let you stay in my place, and never asked for anything. Hell, I even drive you around. I bet you have no clue how much gas cost."

"Like the cost matters to you. Your daddy pays for everything. And if my memory serves me correctly, after every show, I slid you fifteen percent. You call that asking me for nothing?"

"That's business! And at least I have a daddy. What you got? Clearly nobody." She folded her arms across her chest.

Her words came straight for me, but I refused to let them hit me. I nodded my head and walked over to my duffle bag. I dug around in the bottom and pulled out a wad of cash.

"Here, this should cover my short stay. Thanks for everything." I tossed my bag over my shoulder and motioned for the door.

"Where are you going?"

I didn't respond and kept on walking.

Her tone relaxed. "Cream, I'm sorry. Cream, don't leave. I didn't mean what I said. I was just mad."

I opened the front door and she still yelled. It was was time for me to leave, fuck trying not to seem appreciative. I had to get back to what I knew, back to the me I knew.

"You walk out of that door, don't bother coming back! Cream... Cream... Cream!"

SLAM!

"You'll regret it!" she screamed and I heard the door re-open as I jogged down the stairs. "You can't run your whole life!"

SLAM!

Twenty-two

It was back to hotels and I didn't mind. I hated it and loved it; hated it because when I left Payton, I left all my future bookings behind, but loved it because I didn't have somebody breathing down my neck about what I was or wasn't doing. I knew I'd have to disappear on Payton eventually, but I at least thought I'd have a steady flow of money coming in. I had a crazy idea to go back to taking my clothes off for men. Money was money.

The only gig that was guaranteed was my Saturday nights at the gay club. It was cool, but it wouldn't keep enough money in my pocket for transportation, food, room and board, and clothes.

I should have at least packed up all the nice shit that Payton bought for me. I could have sold it. Oh well, it was what it was.

It was already another Saturday, three weeks since I walked out on Payton. I had a gig that night and there was a fifty-fifty chance that I'd run into her at the club. If she had midterms or something to study for, then she wouldn't be there, but if she just wanted to be a bitch and spite me, she'd show her face. Either way, I wasn't going to pay her any mind.

I did like I'd been doing and called up a taxi. I'd been riding in them so often now that I had my own driver, Edwin. He gave me his card one night after dropping me to the club. Even gave me a set rate and told me to call him anytime, on or off the clock. He was a godsend until I could find another chauffer. I seriousy had to get over my fear of driving or I was going to go broke paying somebody else.

Edwin dropped me off at the club. I walked past the long line winking, dapping off studs, and kissing cheeks. I had become quite the celebrity. Truth be told, not everyone liked me. There were studs that gave me the fish eye, pulling their girl closer when I walked by—like their chick was something worth stealing—and femmes that assumed I was stuck up.

As I walked toward the front of the line, I looked out to the lot and at the back, there was a car that looked exactly like Tasia's for the third week in a row. The two weeks before I chalked it up as coincidence, but that night, something just wasn't sitting right. It was parked in the same spot, facing the same direction, almost like it never moved.

I headed inside to prepare for my show. I told myself that if the car was still outside when I left, I would investigate.

I did my thing as usual and instead of leaving early, I hung around for awhile. I needed to build my clientele back up. I exchanged numbers with a few people and talked about some possible gigs. I didn't need a damn manager.

Around two, I decided to head back to my hotel. I left the club and was instantly reminded of my earlier mission when I spotted the familiar car parked to back of the lot. I walked over without caution and just as I thought, Tasia was reclined in her seat, sleeping. I tapped on her window to wake her.

"What are you doing out here?"

She ran her hand over her head. "Oh, um…"

"You okay?"

"Yeah, I'm fine." She sighed and dropped her hands in her lap.

"You've been parked out here for weeks?"

"It's a coping thing. I-I come go back to the places where major life changes occurred… it-it's a coping thing. It helps me to deal and accept it."

"Uh huh," I said and looked into her backseat, which was piled with garbage bags. "Are you living in your car?"

"Cream, it's a long story. Just go home, okay. I'm fine."

"No, you're not. Look, come to my hotel with me."

"No, no, I couldn't." She waved her hand.

"You can. I want you to. I mean, I heard what your friend did, but I still feel partially responsible. I'd feel better if you just came with me, even if its for one night. Please?"

"Hey! You good over there?" I heard my cab driver call out. I forgot that he'd be waiting for me. He must have watched me.

"I'm great, Ed. I don't need a ride tonight. I'll call you."

He nodded and walked away. I turned my attention back towards Tasia. I didn't know what came over me. I felt the need to take care of her and make sure that she was okay. Her resemblence to Kitty made me a different person.

"You're coming with me, right?" I said as more of a demand than a suggestion. She nodded and I ran around to her passenger side so that we could be on our way.

Once we arrived to the hotel, Tasia insisted on keeping her things in her car. I ignored her and drug as much as I could carry up to my room while she followed, dragging her feet and looking down at the ground. It was obvious that she was still going through the storm. I wasn't shocked.

"Are you hungry?" I asked, pushing her bags against the wall in the room.

"No. I'm okay."

"Sleepy?"

She shook her head yes.

"Cool. You can take the bed and I'll just get some extra blankets for the floor or something."

"You don't have to do that."

"Tasia, just get some rest. I'll be good, okay?"

She walked over to the bed and laid down, pulling the covers up to her eyes.

Tasia laid in the same spot for three days. She cried and she held herself. She would get up only to shower then she retook her warm spot in the bed. I couldn't fathom what she was going through. What I did realize as I watched her, was that I'd never mourned anything, not even Kitty. I shed tears, but I never dealt. Never got upset that my parents didn't want me, never cared that girls didn't friend me, never cared that I never really had a home, a sibling, a grandmother... I never let myself care.

I occupied the floor, wanting to respect her space. There weren't many verbal exchanges, only *"Are you hungry"* from me and *"no"* from her. I'd never had to deal with anyone's pain before.

On the fourth day, her agony was just too much to bear. I was starting to feel like I needed to sit and cry with her. I stood over her as she curled in the hotel bed, cuddled with one of the pillows.

"I'll be downstairs in the lobby if you need anything."

I didn't wait for her to nod or budge. I grabbed a notebook and pen, since I hadn't written to Corey in a while and headed out. I sighed with relief once I was on the other side of the door. I rubbed my hand across my head and headed for the elevator. A door squeaked as it opened, but I didn't bother to see where the sound came from.

"Cream?" a raspy voice called out and I turned to see Tasia poking her head out.

"Yes?"

"I think I'm hungry."

"You want to go get something?"

She shook her head no.

"Room service?"

"That'll work."

I spun on my heel and retreated.

Room service was quick. She and I picked over a platter of chicken strips and French fries. She watched the plate and I watched her.

"You want to talk about it?" I asked.

"I don't know what to say exactly."

"Start with how you feel."

"I don't feel anything."

I knew that feeling.

Twenty-three

I tried everything to get Tasia out of that room. I could barely get her close to a window. It was as though she wanted to forget the world existed. It was day nine and she still sobbed, but less painfully now. Her body no longer jerked. She only sniffed. She was breaking me down.

I leaned against the bathroom doorsill with my hands inside of my Walmart sweatpants pockets. I had to try the one thing that was off limits to everyone else.

I cleared my throat. "My real name is Kelli Coursey." My voice cracked. "I was born on February 24th, 1989, and I never knew my parents."

Tasia wiped her eyes and sat up.

"I, uh, grew up in foster care and to keep myself leveled, I read a lot of books. I don't have a favorite color and I've never been to a movie theater… I cant ride a bike… I have a fear of driving and I haven't had a permanent address since eighteen." I fidgeted with my hands now and looked at the floor. "My favorite book is The Bluest Eye... I've never broken a bone," I tapped on the door frame: knock on wood. "And my biggest fear is never knowing who I truly am or where I came from. I keep running and running, but I just feel like I only run into myself."

"Why are you telling me all of this?" Her voice still cracked with old tears.

"I just wanted to distract you from your own life for a little while. Sometimes hearing about someone else's life makes you feel better about yours. I've only told one person everything that I'm telling you. It's nothing too serious, but it's a start."

"Why me?"

"You remind me of her."

"Where is she?"

"She was killed."

Tasia hung her shadowed head. "I'm sorry."

"Don't apologize." I changed the subject to lighten the mood. "So, do you think I can get you into some sunlight today?"

She halfway smiled and nodded her head yes. I knew it was because her pity shifted from herself to me—little, old lost me.

Tasia and I settled for a little bar and grill called The Vortex in Downtown Atlanta. The concierge said it had the best burgers. When we sat down she asked me for twenty singles and I looked at her strangely.

"What do you need twenty ones for?"

"The tip."

"I need you to go a little bit deeper, if I'm giving away twenty dollars."

She laughed and the sound was refreshing after being drubbed with the sound of her distress. "I almost never give away the whole twenty. I stack them in the middle of the table and with everything they do wrong, I deduct a dollar. For exacmple, if a server comes to the table and doesn't introduce themself, I take a dollar, or if they don't refill our drinks after passing and seeing an empty glass, I take a dollar."

"Oh, I get it. That's a cool idea."

"Yeah, I don't know when I started doing it."

I decide to humor her. I handed her twenty singles and she did just as she said. Our server was on point for a while.

She picked at her fries while I inhaled a burger with cheese.

"You know she drugged us?" Tasia said all of a sudden.

"Huh?"

"Lottie. That night at the club when everything went down, she put something in our drinks."

"How'd you find that out?"

"When I went to pick up my things. She gave me a full confession. She had the nerve to have tears in her eyes, begging me to understand that they were in love and really didn't want to hurt me."

"She was your best friend?"

"Best friend and Maid of Honor. This girl stood beside me every step of the way. You would think at some point she would have had the gall to tell me what was up."

"That's exactly why I've only had one friend. People can't be trusted."

"You're right about that." She dipped her fry in ketchup and left it there. "I appreicate you letting me crash your space."

"It's cool. If you don't mind me asking, why were you sleeping in your car?"

"This might sound weird because of what you told me about yourself earlier, but I grew up in foster care too. Only differnce is, I was actually adopted. My parents were abusive though and only did it for the money. When I met Fred, I left everything behind. I was only seventeen and I thought he saved me. He bought me the car I'm driving, moved me into his house, and told me I never had to work. It felt good to tell my parents they weren't worth shit. My mother told me I'd be back. I told her I'd be homeless before I ever went crawling back to her." She sighed. "I stayed in school and graduated and just as Fred promised, he kept taking care of me. Even when I wanted a part time job, he insisted that I relax and rely on him and trust him."

"Damn, and what about this Lottie chick?"

"Oh, Lottie? She and I were friends since middle school. She was all for me leaving my adopted parents' house. She'd witnessed the abuse for herself. Them cussing at me and making me do unneccesary chores for food and clothes... it's so much."

"And your other friends at the club that night?"

"They were Lottie's friends first. I guess you could say it was a package deal. That's why I'm not shocked they lied for her. Their loyalty was never with me."

"So now you have to start all over?" I asked.

She nodded her head yes, slowly, with a somber expression.

"I know that all too well." I took another big bite of my burger. Tasia stared.

"Thank you," she said suddenly.

"For what?"

"All of this. I'm technically a complete stranger to you. Why are you being so nice to me? I mean, I know I remind you of your friend, but there has to be more."

"I'm still figuring it out myself. I'm still silently freaking out at how much you look like her."

"I feel honored," she smirked.

We finished the rest of our food then headed back to the room leaving the waitor with twelve dollars. Somehow she had hit a switch that kept me talking. I told her more about my life, the parts that

163

I knew and remembered: Ms. Weston, Tanisha, her followers, the books I read, the shows I watched, the boys I never dated, the games I never played, and the dances I never attended. It was Kitty déjà vu.

"You own a house?!" Her eyes popped when I got to the story of how I got into taking off my clothes for money.

"Yeah, what's the big deal?"

"That's huge! Why are you jumping from hotel to hotel when you have a deed to a house?"

"I didn't want to be in Kansas anymore. There was nothing there for me."

"What's *here* for you?"

"Money."

"Is that all you care about?" That same question everybody always asked that warranted the same answer.

"What else is there to care about in a world full of liars and cheats?"

"Ms. Weston was one person. There are good people in the world. Kitty was the example of that."

"And she was taken away from me."

"I'm sure she didn't want to leave you, Kelli."

I shivered at the sound of my birth name and it must have showed on my face, too.

"Did I say something wrong?"

"I'm just not used to anyone saying my government name. I haven't answered to it since I left Ms. Weston's authority."

"I won't say it if it makes you uncomfortable."

"I'm okay with it. Just please don't say it in public."

She laughed. "I won't. So when is your next show?"

"Saturday."

"Can I come?"

"You can go wherever you want. It's a free country. If you're comfortable around gay people then by all means, have at it."

"Gay people don't bother me at all. I do have a lot of questions about them though."

"Like what?"

"What's it like?" She looked at me for the answer.

"Don't ask me. I've only been a part of this lifestyle for a little under a year. I'm sure there is more to it than what I can tell you."

"Wait, you've only been gay for a few months?"

"You make it sound bad when you say it like that."

She laughed. "You're not really gay then."

"Why do you say that?"

"In my experience with gay people, they almost always tell you what it is they love about their lifestyle. If you don't have a real appreciation for women then you aren't really gay."

"I know I'm not straight and I do enjoy the sex."

"You can enjoy sex with anyone when it's done right."

165

"So, you would have sex with a woman?"

"Probably. I'm not closed to anything. You only get one life." She shrugged.

"Freak."

We both fell out laughing.

By midnight, Tasia and I lay side by side, face-to-face. Both Cream and Siren had silenced themselves and I was Kelli once again. I was eighteen, nose wide open, and on a path to nothing. I envied people who knew what their future could possibly look like. What I'd done for money in clubs was nothing compared to the cool breezed I felt against my naked emotions.

"I do wonder a lot of things about myself, like where my nose and eyes come from. I wonder why my parents gave me up or if I was taken away. My foster mother always promised to tell me what she knew, but she held the information to keep me doing the things she wanted me to do."

"You loved her, didn't you?"

"Almost."

"Let's talk about love. Have you ever loved anyone, romantically?"

I snarled. "Yeah, right. I don't have a clue what that means and never really cared to find out."

"I don't think that's true. I think you're looking for some kind of love and stability."

"What's so special about either one?"

"What? Is that a trick question? They both are everything. There are so many possibilities with love, and stability keeps you there."

"I swear that sounds like something Kitty would have said."

"Kitty was a smart woman."

"She really was. She was like nobody I'd ever met before."

"She'd be happy to know that you still take care of her brother."

I lowered my eyes.

"You're a good person too, Kelli. This lifestyle that you hide behind... I don't think it's who you are at all."

"Sometimes, I don't believe so either, but when you look the way I do and people give you whatever you want, what else can you say?"

"I agree that you're beautiful, but you have to be deeper than that. You have to."

Twenty-four

"Is this what you do all day when you aren't dancing?" Tasia asked.

"What?"

"Sleep!"

"What should I be doing?"

"Seriously? You've been to all these beautiful places and you don't explore them? This is the 'A' baby. There is plenty to get into."

"You don't see me laying here having the time of my life? I can turn on my side, put my hands behind my head, reach for the remote," I teased.

"Get up. I'm taking you somewhere."

I didn't argue. I got up and dressed. "You're in a good mood for somebody who was depressed for a full week straight."

"Yeah, after finally getting into some air yesterday, I feel new again. Nothing keeps me down for too long."

"Good."

We left for wherever Tasia was taking me. I rode with my seat reclined back and my feet up on her dashboard. I sat up when the car started to slow down. My mouth dropped and excitement overwhelmed me as we pulled into Starlight Six—a drive in movie theater.

"This is a real life drive-in."

"Yep, the only one in Atlanta."

"How are we going to hear the movie?

"A radio channel. It plays through the speakers in the car."

I was fascinated and for the first time I felt like a kid. I sat with my eyes glued to the screen as *Inception* played. Tasia looked over at me every few minutes and I did the same to her. She seemed to be getting a thrill out of the fact that I'd never seen a movie on screen before.

She kept checking her phone while we watched the movie and her expression would change. *He's not coming back and he won't call* was my silent response to her expression.

After the movie, we headed back to the room.

"Did you enjoy it?" she asked.

"Yeah, that was pretty cool."

"Right? See, there is more to the world than clubs."

"Yeah, that requires me to spend money though."

"You didn't think it was worth it?"

I thought about it for a moment. "Yeah, it was worth it."

"Good. Hey, let's not go back to the room. Let's go to the mall."

"For what?"

"Nothing. We can just look around."

"The purpose of the mall is to shop."

"Not all the time. I go to get style ideas. You want to go or not?"

"We can go."

Tasia rerouted for the mall and when we got there, it was packed. She took me to the exact same mall that Payton had taken me to. We walked from store to store, putting together outfits and talking about people who clearly had no sense of fashion.

After we got tired of walking, we went to the food court and rested.

"Can I ask you a question?" Tasia queried.

"Uh huh."

"What's with the name changes?"

"Funny you ask that." I laughed. "I used to be a femme."

"A femme?"

"Yeah, I dressed and acted like you."

"Okay, sooo what are you now?"

"A stud."

She laughed. "Are you kidding me. What the hell is that?"

"Me, I guess. The girl I came here with told me this look better suited me."

"Hmm, I think you'd look good either way. You have very unique features. A lot of people can't flip-flop like that and pull it off. I can definitely see you in makeup. You should let me do your face."

"You can." I smiled.

"Even though you look good the way you are, the baggy clothes thing is kind of played out."

"You don't like what I have on?" I looked down at my oversized jeans and t-shirt.

"If you were going for the corner-boy look then I'd feel you, but, uh, for who you are and what you do, it won't work."

"You have something else in mind?"

"Let's go." Tasia stood from the table and we rejoined the walking crowd.

We walked in and out of men's and women's clothing stores. Taisa had undone the style Payton created for me. She actually let me decide what I liked and didn't like and by the end of the day, I even had a favorite color—yellow.

I left the mall with at least twelve bags.

"You mind telling me why you walk around with $2,000 dollars on you?"

"I don't have a bank card and you never know what could happen," I said as we headed to the car.

"You could get robbed, that's what could happen."

"Wouldn't be the first time. I was robbed when I first started dancing back in Kansas."

"You say it like it's okay."

"What can I do about it? It happened. He didn't kill me, just took the measly three hundred I was walking around with."

"You are a strange person," she laughed, but stopped abrutly along with her steps. Her eyes bulged. I looked up to see what she was focused on. Fred and Lottie were hand-in- hand, moving in our direction, happy as could be, at the sacrifice of Tasia's heart.

I placed my hand on her back. "Come on. They deserve each other."

Her feet moved reluctantly and she kept her eyes on the two people who'd broken her. They spotted her and slowed in their steps.

All three of them knew that they weren't ready to confront each other again. The wounds were still too fresh. Fred and Lottie alternated through cars and I dragged Tasia in the opposite direction.

"You okay?" I asked once we made it to her car.

"I will be. It's just hard. That man told me that he loved me for years. He did anything for me, and he pretended to be so excited about marrying me and this whole time, it was all a lie."

"You aren't going to go back to the room and start this depressing stage all over again, are you?"

She shook her head no.

"Good, because we have things to do." She kept her head down. "Tasia, look at me." She looked up. "I've told you my secrets and I know you have trust issues right now, but know that I won't let you drown, okay? We'll tread water together. If one sinks, so will the other."

She forced a smile and nodded her head in agreement.

"Stop blinking," Tasia said as she attemped to line my eyes.

I agreed to let her color on my face just to keep her mind off her low-life ex-fiance and her backstabbing ex-best friend. We stopped at a store and she purchased stupid board games and junk food.

"Remember when I asked you about love?"

"Yeah."

"Think you'll ever love someone?"

"I'm not sure. You think you'll ever love again?"

"I know I will," she confirmed.

"How are you so sure?"

"I'm just built that way. No matter what happens to me in life, I need to love."

"Even after what your fiance did?"

"Even after him. It was messed up, but when it was good, it was the best."

"It was a lie. You said it yourself."

"Lies feel so good. You have to go through it to understand. What you don't know, truly can't hurt you. He may not have loved me, but I loved him and that alone keeps my conscience clear and keeps me capable of loving, because I did what I was supposed to do. I'm not the broken one, he is. I just deserve better."

"I want to be like you when I grow up," I teased and we both laughed. Tasia was one of those rare irreplacable people in life. "You know what I just thought about?"

"What?"

"I told you stuff about me and you didn't really return the favor, other than telling me about being adopted."

"Oh, what do you want to know?"

"The basics are good."

"Well, my birthday is July 10th. I'm actually three years older than you."

"You're twenty-four?"

She laughed. "Yeah. You say it like you don't believe it."

"I do. I guess I just think everyone I meet is twenty-one."

"That's not special at all," she said with a hint of sarcasm in her tone.

"Keep going."

"All right. My favorite color is purple," she said and then paused. "This just feels really juvenile." She smiled.

"How?"

"I don't know. I feel like this is a conversation I'd be having on the phone at thirteen."

"It's okay to be a little juvenile sometimes. I find myself being that way often since I grew up so quickly. That nostalgia that you feel with this conversation… I don't feel it. I didn't gossip on the phone, go to dances, chase boys, and all that."

174

"Why are you a stripper, Kelli?" she aked, dropping her makeup brush and hands from my face.

"What do you mean?"

"I've listened to you speak every day. You are clearly intelligent. I mean, who says nostalgia?" she laughed. "You are clearly intellectual when you're not secretive. Is there anything else you would have been in life?"

I looked her in her eyes. "You want to talk about dreams now?"

"I do. Tell me." She leaned closer.

I took a breath. "I wanted to be a foster parent, once upon a time. There was this little girl that Ms. Weston received when she got rid of the girl I had a problem with. She was only six months and her parents had beaten her and thrown her against a wall. It was the first time I could rememeber crying. I-I just wanted to take care of her. Her real parents had the nerve to fight to get her back. It was sickening. I wanted to be a parent to kids who didn't ask to be in this world, but were here anyway and had to grow up thinking it was their fault."

"Children like you?" she asked.

"And you."

We looked away from one another.

"So, why didn't you follow that path?" She spoke for the pink elephant in the room.

"My path was chosen for me."

Twenty-five

As the weeks went on, she came to my shows—even helped me to get booked for more parties. She set up a show booking, via email, for me and responded to them without my asking. She'd replaced Payton and didn't ask for fifteen percent. She figured it was the least she could do, since she was practically living off of me and I'd never even hinted for her to get out. Not that it was my place to put someone out of a hotel anyway.

Tasia showed me her city: the good, the bad, and the ugly.

We visited sex shops, and there I learned that she had a kinky side. She pointed out handcuffs and sex swings and named all the things that she wanted to try. Some of it made me blush and I realized how much more I still had to learn about sex.

Six flags was next on our agenda. I was a punk ass, afraid to get on any of the rides, but after some convincing I just went ahead. The rides were fun, but I got addicted to bumper cars and playing rip-off games for stuffed animals I'd never win. I did eventually get a little Tweety Bird from shooting basketball. I went home with a framed picture of myself screaming for dear life on a rollercoaster.

The Underground reminded me of the Riverwalk in New Orleans, only with more shops. I liked how dark it was inside and the fact that it was actually underground. That day, we also stumbled across a little festival that was happening in the opening right next door. We listened to music and purchased unnecessary things from booths.

We drove past the Georgia Dome, visited the zoo and aquarium, and walked Centennial Olympic Park.

But even with all of that, it was the King Center, National Historic Site, that took my breath away. We visted the home of Martin Luther King's birth, Ebenezer Baptiste church, and his tomb. I had never had so much respect for one person until that day. I left overwhelmed and in tears.

It touched me so much that I wrote to Corey about it. It made me want to help him fight harder for his appeal. I wanted to make a difference.

"You all right over there?" Tasia asked as I sat at the desk writing to Corey.

"Yeah."

"Just making sure. You haven't said much since we left the museum."

"I know. That was just a lot to take in."

"You weren't taught black history in school?"

177

"They taught us what they wanted us to know."

I was an emotional wreck that entire day. And with those feelings came thoughts of all the happenings between Tasia and I. I felt haunted by her, and not in the creepy I-see-dead-people kind of way. But in the your-spirit-will-always-live-on kind of way. I sat and watched her as she walked back and forth through our room.

I said "our".

She tussled with her hair, pulling it up into a messy bun, then she flopped down on the bed and opened her laptop. Tasia meant more to me than I realized; it dawned on me.

She was always on my mind, from her smile to her voice. When I shopped, I found myself looking at things I thought she'd like and sometimes I'd get them for her. Somehow, I was finding happiness in her happiness.

I wondered if that was what it felt like to belong to somebody. I started to change my ways, backing out of gigs with women I'd slept with. That included Baltimore and Miami, because I knew that Ana and Gabriella lived in those places. I knew that I'd have sex with them and for some reason I didn't really care to anymore.

When I had local shows, I needed to see Tasia in the crowd. If I didn't find her right away, I got angry. Then I got upset at myself for being angry for no damn reason.

I could say that I loved her, but I wasn't exactly sure what that feeling entailed. I knew what it meant to love someone as a friend or as a family member, but romantically? I had no clue. How was I even worthy of such a feeling?

Get it together, Cream. Get it together.

I couldn't keep this to myself. I added to the letter that I wrote to Corey. I told him about Tasia and the resemblance she had to Kitty. I convinced myself that my vulnerability with her was only because of the fact that she looked so much like someone I truly cared about. What other reason could there be? Corey would either think I was sick or tease me.

"Uh, Kelli. I think you should look at this."

"What is it"

"Come read it."

I sat my ink pen down on my desk. I took Tasia's laptop and looked for what she was talking about.

"No this bitch didn't," I said.

"Who is that?"

I reread the comment under my YouTube video again, then clicked on the account that it belonged to. It was exactly who I thought it was. Payton was going under all of my videos and saying that I had an STD. And I quote, "I don't know why people even go crazy about this bitch. She isn't all of that anyway. She fucks anything that walks and she's not that good at it."

Payton had taken down her picture but forgot to remove the old videos of me dancing. So much for being anonymous. I happily replied.

"You aren't going to entertain that are you?" Tasia asked.

"Watch me."

I didn't hold back as I let everybody who repsonded to her know that she was a trick and if I had an STD, then she gave it to me. I told the whole story of why she was bitter and handed the laptop back to Tasia.

"Was she your previous manager?" Tasia asked as she read the comment I posted.

"Yeah, that's her."

"Wow, she's really mature."

"Can you believe she goes to Spelman?"

"Acting like this?"

"Exactly."

"Well, I don't think she will have anything else to say after this." Tasia laughed.

"She's just a spoiled bitch. She's not used to being told no."

"I'm staying out of that. I have shows to book. You still don't want me to respond to this Gabriella chick?"

My chest tightened. I didn't know what it was, but suddenly I felt the need to go to Florida. "Tell her I'll do the show."

T wenty-six

I dreamed I was making love to a faceless woman. It felt so real. I knew that it was a dream, but my body reacted to it outside of my slumber. Tasia was lying beside me.

The dream came alive to me as I shifted my sleep. I rolled over to where Tasia laid and slid my hands beneath the t-shirt that she wore. I fondled her nipple until it hardened. I heard her moan, thinking it was the woman in my dream.

"Kelli," she whispered and I pulled her closer, pressing my lips to her neck and doing to her all the things that I did to this woman in my sleep. I never opened my eyes and Tasia never stopped me.

"Kelli," she whispered again as my fingers crept down between the warmth of her thighs and slid between the crease of her lips.

"What are you doing?" she whisper-moaned and I fondled her clit. "Kelli, wake up." She reached for me.

It was her cold hand to the back of my neck that made me realize what I was doing. I opened my eyes and it was too late to stop now. Tasia bit down on her bottom lip.

"I've never done this before."

Her words excited me and I now felt what Payton did when she learned that I'd never been touched.

Although I knew that Tasia was not pure in that department, I was turned on by the fact that I'd be the first woman. I should have stopped myself, but I couldn't. The begging in her eyes kept me there.

"Kiss me," she whispered.

Fully aware now, I leaned up and pressed my hands beside her, mounted over her. Our breathing collided. I looked down and she looked up. I knew that if I did this, things wouldn't be the same in the morning, but I'd already gone so far. Payton was the first person I kissed, but then, my heart didn't pound the way it did at that moment with Tasia. Kissing wasn't my thing. I wasn't even sure I was that good at it since my experience level was at one. But who was I to say no to *her*.

I almost—just almost—removed myself, but she reached up and her hands melted against me; they seemed native to my skin, unlike the women who touched me before. I knew they were temporary. I knew they'd never be *mine*. In that little motion, that one gesture of her welcoming touch, I could tell the difference. Other women pulled at me with lust. They weren't gentle. They didn't take their time and they damn sure didn't care about how I felt. They just wanted me to get into their sacred place, learn enough to appease them, and get out, but not Tasia. According to the longing in her expression, she wanted me to go in and stay and scrutinize for as long as we both could take it.

She bent her neck, slightly, meeting me half way and waiting for me to meet her request.

I lowered my lips to her lips and was drunken by her kiss. I followed her lead, sucking at her bottom lip when she sucked on my top, then we'd trade.

Shit.

Dammit.

Cream, stop yourself right now. Right now! But it feels so damn good.

I was at war with myself. I pulled away.

"I can't do this to you. You aren't gay," I whispered. I needed an excuse. But she wouldn't let me have one.

"You either, rememeber?" She smiled.

"Yes I am."

"Then appreciate me," she said, tugging at my t-shirt and pulling it over my head. She was right about what she'd said before. I'd never appreciated a woman before. I recognized their beauty, took them for what they could do—what they were good for, but I never saw them as people who, like me, could easily be broken, needed love, time, and attention.

Didn't care about the curve of their lips, the batting of their eyes, the time they took to dress. I paid no mind to the softness of their hands, the scent of their hair and body, the hardness of their

183

nipples, or the taste of their breath. I ignored the gentleness of their words, the kindness of their hearts, and sometimes the invisibility of their pride. Women were unique creatures. Lovable ones. I decided to make up for my lack of appreciation of all the women in that moment, on that night.

I took appreaciation for its most literal meaning. I appreciated her breasts, sucking them one by one, squeezing them in my hands. I appreciated her fingers, her ears, her neck, her shoulders, her stomach, the inside of her navel, the heaving of her chest, the tremor of her body, the heat of her insides, and the crease where her vagina and her thighs met.

Most of all, I appreciated her pussy. I appreciated it so much that I wrapped my mouth around it, pulled at the skin and tickled the hardness in the middle with my tongue. I appreciated it until it came all over the bed.

T wenty-seven

The person I knew myself to be and the person that I was becoming started to clash after that night of sex, no, lovemaking, no, sex with Tasia.

I found myself living two different lives. During the week, I was a door-opening, pillow-talking, cuddling, somewhat relationship type stud. On the weekends, I was a hoe.

Tasia clung to me more and there started to be more feelings of "relationship" than friendship.

There were dinner dates, more movie trips, and hand-holding, which I tried to avoid by pretending my palms were sweaty. She would kiss me randomly, nothing obscene, just a peck here and there on the lips, neck, or cheek.

I had to get away.

Gabriella booked me once again in Miami, and like usual, after the show, we went back to her place. I needed to do this to keep myself from whatever it was that Tasia had over me. Now I remembered why I needed to say yes to her event. To me, this was keeping myself balanced between loving and not.

Love would have stopped me, right?

"You already know what I want, Gabriella said, biting her lip and backing up to her bed.

I dropped the jeans I wore, exposing the new strap that I wore; one-hundred and fifty dollars for a damn toy. I was going to make every penny worth it, right between her legs.

"Turn around and bend over," I commanded and like a good girl, she did what she was told.

"I want all of it, Papi."

"And you'll get it," I said, moving closer, then inserting the tip of it inside of her.

"Mmmm," she moaned and instantly I felt that what I was doing was wrong. I felt that I was cheating on Tasia.

I shook it off and kept on going, closing my eyes and focusing on Gabriella.

"Fuck me, Kelli."

"What did you just call me?" I paused.

"Cream. Now keep going."

I pumped slowly, but I knew I heard my name. How would she even know it? I eased out and pushed her down on the bed, making her lie on her back, so that I could get on top. All I did was blink my eyes and she was Tasia laying before me, reaching for me, pulling my body on hers, locking her fingers with mine and lifting her neck a little to meet me halfway to kiss me. I pushed her in her face.

"What is wrong with you?" Gabriella sat up.

"I-I-don't know."

"You wiggin' for real."

"I'm sorry," I said.

"Are you not into this? Because if you're not, I can take you back to your room?"

"I'm good. Let's do this."

I wasn't good, but I dared not have a woman telling anybody that I didn't deliver. I held my head up, pushed her knees to her chest and gave her what she wanted. A good beating. Images of Tasia still plagued me, but I tried my damnedest to shake them off and keep on going until Gabriella came.

I thought it would stop with her, but it didn't. The back and forth continued and I tried to split myself in two. I was going crazy. Every woman was Tasia. I had clearly crossed a line with her that I shouldn't have, and now I had to deal with the consequence.

"What are you thinking about?" Tasia asked as we lay in bed. I faced the wall and her arm was wrapped around me.

"Nothing."

"You have to be thinking about something."

"Nope, nothing."

"Absolutely nothing? Or you just don't want to share?"

Option two. "Um, I have a song stuck in my head," I lied.

"What song is it?"

"Usher, Hot Tottie."

She giggled. "Why that song?"

"I'm trying to picture myself doing a show to it."

"It's has a hot beat. I think you'd kill it. Now tell me what's really on your mind." Her tone changed. I hoped she didn't feel my heart jump.

"What makes you think that's not it?"

"Kelli, you put a pillow between us when you got in the bed and you haven't really touched me, in that way, since the first time we had sex. Was I bad at it? Tell me something."

"Take your foot off my neck. Why does something have to be bothering me. Can't I just have some quiet moments. Who pays attention to all that shit anyway?"

"Wow." Tasia took a deep breath I assumed to gather herself. It was my guilty conscience that made me overreact, but I couldn't tell her that.

"Can you just say what's on your mind? I can't fix whatever it is if you don't talk to me," she pushed.

"Just drop it."

Tasia pulled her arms from my body and replaced the pillow that was originally there, giving me the space that I needed. I closed my eyes and dozed off to sleep.

Twenty-eight

Tasia was only angry for that night. She went back to her loving self the very next morning, but me, I still strayed. I was trying to disconnect myself from this confusion, this internal source of bewilderment.

A few weeks later, she tried again.

"You want to talk about what happened?" Tasia asked as I packed my bags to dance in Vegas for the weekend.

I shook my head no.

"Did I do something wrong?"

"Tasia, no."

"I'm not trying to agitate you. I'm just curious since you've been tip-toeing around me. Something has been wrong for weeks. I just ignored it, but I can't anymore. I don't like—"

"Look, I'm just not used to this, okay?"

"Used to what?"

"Feeling like I'm in a relationship. I feel like since we had sex, now you expect something more from me."

"Did I ever hint at wanting more?"

"No."

"Okay then, why are you assuming? I know you've never been committed before, Kelli. Shit, up until a few months ago, I couldn't even get you to sleep in the bed. It wasn't marriage, it was sex. I'm not some needy idiot that assumes because somebody fucks me that we're in love. You could give me more credit."

"You may not have said it, but you suggest it everytime you cuddle up next to me or reach for my hand when we walk out in public. You've been doing it for the last two weeks."

"I can't be affectionate?"

"You weren't doing it before."

She rolled her eyes and grabbed her car keys. "I'll meet you at the car." Tasia left the room and slammed the door behind her.

I could be exaggerating. It was Payton that had me all messed up. I grabbed my bag and went down to the car where Tasia sat with sunglasses on, tapping her thumb against the steering wheel. The music was low at first, but when I got in and attemped to apologize, because I didn't want her mad at me anymore, she turned up the volume and pulled off.

Usually when Tasia dropped me off at the airport, she would park in the garage and walk with me all the way to security. That day, she dropped me off and didn't look my way.

191

"See you when you get back," she said and pulled off. I didn't want her pissed at me, but I knew it was my fault for making her actions out to be more than what they were.

My flight from Atlanta to Vegas was four hours and four minutes. The time difference between the two made it seem like the clock only moved for an hour. I slept every second. One of the promoters for the event was already at the airport waiting for me. I'd also had sex with her the last time I was there and from the look on her face as I approached, she had the same expectation.

Before, I'd be all over the oppurtunity, but this time something was different. I didn't lust for her at all. Yvette was a beautiful femme that shared the same complexion as me: chocolate that melted in your mouth and not in your hand. She wore her hair short in the same cut as Meagan Good and she was petite, which made her easy to toss around a bedroom.

"You look well rested." Yvette smiled.

"I slept the entire flight."

"You want to come back to my place or go straight to your room?" she asked. From the way she phrased the question, I could tell her hope was in me going back to her place.

"I just want to chill in my room."

"That's cool," she said, her tone dripping with disappointment.

She dropped me off and every hour on the hour, she was texting to see if I needed anything. I figured she was checking to see if I changed my mind about leaving my room. I planned on doing my show and bringing my ass back to Atlanta.

I lay in the hotel bed with my hands behind my head, looking up at the ceiling. I wanted to get Tasia off of my mind, but there was no way that I could. It bothered me that I left with her being angry with me.

I pushed myself up from the bed and walked over to the mirror. I started to talk to myself. "Get over yourself," I said then lightly slapped the side of my face.

A part of me wanted to give in to whatever it was that Tasia was offering and the other half of me knew that I just needed to run. It was another city that I'd spent way too much time in. I didn't want another person in my life that could be taken away from me like Kitty was.

I dug into my pocket and texted Yvette. I needed a disconnect from the world for a little while and I could get that between her legs. She would get her wish.

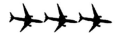

Calling Yvette was much more than I bargained for. She returned to my hotel with three other girls in the car with her, all hungry for me. I got in and asked no questions.

Clothes flew off the moment we walked through the door. The girls passed bottles of liquor around, not bothering to drink from cups.

One of them walked over to me and stood behind me, rubbing her hands down my chest. I didn't have an attraction to her at all, but I'd already put it on my mind to fuck them all, even her.

She pulled my earlobe into her mouth then traced it with her tongue. "You want a drink?"

"No, I'm good," I said, watching as another girl walked over to the stereo and turned on a CD.

"Cream, come over here," Yvette said and patted the couch pillow beside her. I joined her.

She ran her hands across the crotch of my jeans and, in seconds, shit turned pornographic. Yvette rode my strap while I fingered another girl. The other two 69'd on the floor.

They all took turns getting a feel of me then Yvette got bossy, still wanting special attention even though company was her idea. She bent over the sofa and I gave her the attention she craved while one of her friends kissed and licked all over my back.

Each of them waited for me to make them cum and I did just that, making them all pass out one by one, except for Yvette. That girl never got tired. She was satisfied though.

She went to her room and retrieved a robe and we both went into the kitchen. She grabbed two bottles of water from the fridge and handed one to me.

"My body needed that," Yvette said and sat down at the table. "Who taught you how to use a strap like that?"

"I was a natural."

"You keep doing that and I'll have to move you here and wife your ass."

I snapped my head in her directon.

"You the kind of stud that girls fall in love with," she winked.

"Girls don't even know anything about me."

"What do they need to know when you put it down the way you do. You definitely fuck as good as you dance." She smiled.

"Is that all femmes care about?" I asked, sounding foreign to myself.

"No, but it's definitely a huge part. Well, at least to me."

I got up from the bed and began dressing. "Can you take me back to my room?"

"You can get dressed for the show here."

"I think I'm just going to cancel and go to the airport."

"What?"

"You heard me."

"You can't do that."

"I can and I am. You've probably had every stud entertainer you booked digging in your shit."

"Excuse me?"

"You got a hearing problem or something? It's broads like you that make women like Tasia work overtime."

"Who is Tasia? What the fuck are you talking about?"

I grabbed my things and headed for the door. I just wanted to lash out at somebody, anybody.

I looked around at the other girls sprawled out on the floor and wondered what made me any different from them.

In my mind... not a damn thing.

I had to pay close to four hundred dollars just to get on the next flight to Atlanta. On top of the forty I paid for a taxi since Yvette was still cussing at me and refused to take me anywhere.

I didn't bother to call Tasia to pick me up from the airport. I called Edwin and he was more than happy to return me to my room since he hadn't seen me in awhile.

Tasia was in bed when I walked through the door. I debated on joining her, but then I figured it was best to just leave her alone—for good. I'd never be anything more than who I was, lost. I pulled out a sheet of paper and used the light from my cell phone to write her a letter. I dug around in the bottom of my bag for the cash I vowed to never spend. I always said I was saving it for something and this had to be the something. Tasia could use it more than me. It was close to ten-thousand dollars. I walked over to the nightstand and sat it down with the letter. As I walked closer, she turned over in the bed.

"Read it to me."

"Huh?" I said, stalling.

"The runaway letter you just sat beside me. Read it to me."

I stood and I swallowed the lump that formed in my throat. I turned to face Tasia and she sat up in the bed. All that showed in the dark room was her silouette.

"You just want to walk out on me, Kelli?"

I was frozen.

"I know what happened in Vegas. Yvette wasted no time sending you a hate email. I'm not mad. Did you do that because you thought I'd react? You do know that I'd never try to change you, don't you?"

"That wasn't the reason."

"I understand your actions. Cream's actions, Siren's actions, Kelli's actions… I know your bag is packed and you're ready to leave and if that's what you want to do, I won't stop you. I do want to tell you something though. I was just like you. I kept losing people I loved. I wondered why my parents never loved me, never wanted me. I buried my past and my pain and every chance that I got, I disappeared. I had to realize, for myself, that that was just life. We are all dealt a hand of cards. And you and me? We got the most fucked up ones."

Kitty too, I thought.

"…but we have a choice, Kelli. I chose the latter. I refused to be a victim of my circumstances and blame everybody but myself for my unhappiness. Yes, a man cheated on me and left me for my bestfriend, but it led me right here to you. That made the pain worth it, or at least I thought it did. This might make you run full speed ahead, but I love you, Kelli Coursey. Not Siren or Cream, but Kelli, the person that you showed me and no one else. The person that you keep fighting."

The mattress squeaked and I knew that she stood up.

"How can you ever truly find your identity if you won't even accept your name? I won't let you drown. Remember that?"

I could hear the tears forming in her voice. I was happy that I couldn't see her face. For the first time, I actually cared. I cared that it was my fault that someone other than me was hurting. I couldn't play victim here. I sent the signals, giving her pieces of me, then tried to take them back. It wasn't fair.

I squeezed the strap of my bag, hoping that the pressure being applied somewhere else would delay my own tears. I wanted to respond, but I knew myself. Even if I did stay, one day, I'd leave and she'd be destroyed. It was better to get it over with right then. I stepped backwards, pivoted and then headed for the door. It wasn't even latched completely before I fell to my knees and broke down crying. I pressed my back against the door and the tears I held in for twenty-one years soaked my face. I banged my fist against the floor and my head against the door.

"Fuck, fuck, fuck!" I cried as everything that ever affected me in life attacked me all at once, making me a blubbering mess. The door eased opened behind me and Tasia's arms wrapped around me.

"Shhhhh," she said, consoling me. I turned and curled into her and just like that my mind had changed. I was going to stay.

Kitty said it. She said love would hit me.

T wenty-nine

That next weekend, I prepared for my show in Atlanta. Tasia sat in the bed in leggings and a bra, sifting through emails. Things were still heavy between us, but whatever it was that we shared, it was deep.

"That can wait until tomorrow. Get dressed," I said.

"I think you need to read this," she said, a look of concern masked her face.

"If it's another comment from Payton just delete it and block her."

"Kelli. Come. Read." She turned the laptop to face me and I walked over to the bed.

From:rawentertainment@gmail.com
To:bookingsforcream@yahoo.com

Wassup Siren,

I mean, Cream. I see you going by a new name now. I found you on YouTube. Don't ask me what I was searching for, because I'm not even sure.

Anyway, this is Barry. My mama died three months ago and I've been trying to find a way to contact you forever. You meant what you said when you said you were going to fall off the face of the Earth. My mama left a package for you. I know she wasn't your favorite person, but she marked this as priority and made me promise that you'd get it. If you can just send me an address, I'll be sure to get it to you. I'll overnight it to kill some of the anticipation. I hope you're doing well for yourself wherever you are. I have no doubt that you're fine. Any man would pay top dollar just for your company.

Hope to hear from you soon,
Barry Weston

What the hell could she possibly have for me? I hit the response key, keeping the message short and sweet. I'm fine yada-yada and this is my address. Tasia watched me curiously.

"What do you think it is?" she asked.

"Who knows. Knowing that woman, it could be a bomb since I kept that deed for so many years."

She laughed. "I doubt she'd wait this long to blow you up."

"Why not? She'd get away with it since she passed."

"True," she cracked up. "I'm going get dressed."

Tasia and I pulled up to the club. We hopped out and walked in hand-in-hand. I didn't complain so much about her affection. I still had not said those three words that she said to me, but I was coming around and dealing with the permanence of my feelings. I had to admit that Tasia looked good walking beside me. It was almost as if we were made for each other, but who was to say?

She released my hand once inside and I headed to the back to get dressed. My show that night was dedicated to Tasia. I didn't care if I made a single dollar.

Showing my affection to Tasia so openly actually had the opposite effect once my show started. I grinded against her, kissing her every now and then and mouthing the lyrics against her lips. She smiled the whole time. As I walked in a circle around her, I noticed eyes on me, angry ones.

Payton stood with her arms across her chest and her eyes directly on me, making sure not to miss a move. *Aw shit, bring on the drama.* I tried my darndest not to look in her direction for the rest of the performance, but she made sure that I knew she was watching. She rolled her eyes and moved wherever I went.

Once the music stopped, I changed and rejoined Tasia. We stood towards the back of the club, drinks in hand and laughed at the sights. Payton took it upon herself to stay within five to ten feet of us for the remainder of the night. She had a knock-off version of me walking behind her and falling at her feet. I assumed she was breaking her off too.

"Do you know her?" Tasia asked.

"That's Payton. Ms. Youtube."

"No wonder she keeps giving us the eye."

"She'll be all right. Spoiled heifer just mad because she finally found something in life that she can't buy."

Tasia and I laughed.

We stayed until the club closed, dancing to the few slow songs that they played. Tasia was a little tipsy when we left.

"Cream!" A voiced yelled as we headed to the car in the lot.

I swung around, already aware of who it was. I knew she was going to have to say something to me. Her flunky of a stud was right behind her.

"Long time," she said.

"Yeah."

"How you been?"

"Better."

She looked Tasia up and down. "You should come visit me sometime."

"I'll pass on that."

"Damn, why all the attitude?"

"Look Payton, I just want to go home. I'm not in the mood for drama. I don't know why you're standing here like I didn't know it was you with the drama online."

"Drama? Wow. I pay to get you here, put you on in the community and I can't even come say hello without you thinking I'm trying to start something? And that comment was old. I didn't even respond again."

"Yeah, because there was nothing else to be said. What do you want, Payton?"

"To be acknowledged. You seem to have forgotten who made you."

"Made me?"

"Yeah, *made*. I bought your clothes, drove you around—"

"You can kill all that noise." I held my hand up in her face. "I was taking care of myself long before you decided to be a trick. And everything you got me, I left right with you. The shirt your girl has on sure does look familiar."

"Well, you didn't want it. And a trick?"

"Come on, Cream." Tasia tugged at my arm, trying to diffuse what she saw as an escalation. I turned to leave with Tasia.

"What's so special about her? Huh? Cream!"

"You just disrespect me?" Was the last thing that I heard as I walked away. The stud obviously felt some type of way and they started arguing in the parking lot as we left.

Payton threw her shoe at the back of Tasia's car and, for the third time, I gave kudos to Tasia for being a woman and letting it fly.

Thirty

Kelli,

I'm sure I'm the last person that you want to hear from, but when I go, I want to go with a clear conscience. First, I'd like to apologize for what I did to you. I had no right to use you the way that I did. I was an adult and I should have handled my own problems like one. You were only a child. I understand why you did what you did when you left with the deed to my house. It took me years to admit that I was selfish, but once I finally did, I felt free. Now with that said, I remember making you a promise. I told you that I'd get you the truth about your parents. The files don't tell you everything, but I know someone who can. Your mother's name is Minnie Coursey. I couldn't get a phone number on her, but her address is:

2865 Shepperton Terrace
Silver, Spring, MD 20904

I hope that you will use this information to fill in the holes in your life and find the same peace that I did. Again, I am truly sorry.

Sincerely,
Terrilyn Weston

My hands shook as they held on to the piece of paper that held my indentity, my history. Tasia rubbed my back.

"What do you want to do?" she asked.

"What am I supposed to do with this?"

Tasia took the letter from my hands and placed it to the side. She grabbed my hands and kneeled before me. "Whatever you decide to do, I'm behind you. If you want to toss this and keep on living, I'm with you."

"All my life I wanted answers, and now that I can get them, I can't even think of a question."

"That's no biggie. I'll help you come up with some. I'll do whatever you need me to."

I huffed. "What if I go and she slams the door in my face?"

"That'll be her loss."

I squeezed Tasia's hands and took several breaths. "I'm going."

A smile stretched across her face. "When do you want to go?"

"Can you look up flights for tomorrow?"

"Seriously?"

"Yes. If I don't do it now, then I won't. And I need to ask you something."

A look of worry took over. "What?"

"Will you come with me? As my girlfriend?"

I'd never seen a person switch expressions so quickly. Now shock faced me. "Do you know what you're asking?"

"I'm well aware. You told me to start living and stop exisiting, so help me. Do this with me and be with me."

"Kelli—"

"Only if you're ready to commit again." I looked her in her eyes, every part of me shivering. "I love you." I'd never ever said those words. Never. Ever.

"If you want me you got me. I'll go anywhere with you as whoever you want me to be."

We kissed and she released my hands and retrived her laptop.

I let Tasia do what she did best while my nerves got the best of me. *Did I really want to do this? What would I call her? Mom? Minnie? Ms. Coursey? She had my last name. Will she look like me? Or, me like her since she's older?* The room was spinning.

All the times I did shows in Maryland, I never would have guessed my birth mother resided there.

"Okay, I booked us two first class tickets, a room, and a rental."

"How'd you get a rental? Don't you have to be twenty-five for that?"

"Enterprise let's you rent under twenty-five, it's just an extra twenty-five a day."

"I don't know if I can do this."

"Think of it as a beginning. Whether this visit goes great or terribly wrong, you'll know which way to start your life."

"I hope so."

"Pack a bag. Our flight leaves at six in the morning."

I didn't sleep at all. I tossed and I turned while Tasia slept soundly. It was a nervous waiting, like sitting in a court room waiting for jurors to decide your fate. I needed that not-guilty verdict and I needed it now.

I decided to force sleep and just as I did, the alarm on my phone went off. It was four a.m. and we needed to get up. The Hartsfield-Jackson Airport was not the airport you wanted to play around with when you had to catch trains to get to your terminal.

We brushed our teeth and grabbed our bags. I didn't care what people said about us traveling in our pajamas. I had enough to think about.

Edwin was waiting outside of our hotel when we got downstairs. He took our bags and we were on our way.

"I was thinking..." Tasia said.

"Thinking what?"

"How would you feel if we moved into an apartment when we got back? You don't have to answer now, just think about it."

I nodded.

"Something else, too, but it doesn't have anything to do with us."

"What is it?"

"I'm thinking about going to school. You know getting a degree and a job. You can't take care of me forever."

"Will that make you happy?"

"It would."

"Then I have your back."

Tasia smiled as if she had just gotten my permission rather than told me what it was she was planning to do. Perhaps she needed validation.

"Are you nervous?"

"Yes, what's with the rambling?"

"I don't know. I guess I didn't realize I needed to be prepared to support you. I might have booked this too soon for the both of us."

"Now you say something."

"We can turn around."

"And let over a thousand dollars go towards a credit? It's too late for that."

"Yeah, you're right. I'll be quiet now."

I laughed. Her rambling was actually putting me at ease. I'd never seen her nervous before.

Edwin pulled up to the airport and I thought, *it's now or never.* In one hour and thirty-nine minutes, I'd be close to the woman who birthed me and gave me up, possibly.

T hirty-one

Silver Spring, Maryland

We checked in, retrieving our tickets then went through security. Tasia was silent, but she touched me every so often to make sure that was okay.

I slept through the flight; a little rest was better than none. We picked up our rental car and GPS'ed our way to our hotel. We got an early check-in and when I got to the room, I didn't want to leave.

"What is a decent time to visit someone's house?"

"That's a good question."

"This is so screwed up."

"Just get dressed."

"What if she doesn't like gay people?"

"Kelli, get dressed. We'll have some breakfast and find a mall if you want to change."

"I'm not changing for her!" I grew agitated for no reason at all.

Tasia walked over to me and pulled me into her arms. "You need to relax."

"I'm trying to. I just don't know what I'm even doing here. What can she possibly tell me to make everything okay?"

"You don't know and neither do I, but I do know you will pop a vein if you don't chill out."

I got dressed and Tasia and I found a little place to eat in an area where everything was written in Chinese, even McDonalds, but you couldn't miss those golden arches.

After filling our bellies, it was time to follow the recorded voice on the GPS to my mother's house. *My mother.*

After damn near thirty minutes, maybe longer, we pulled up to a townhouse community. Tasia parked and I looked around. A few kids were outside, but that was it.

"You want me to come with you?"

"No, I need to do this on my own."

I told myself that I was ready several times, but I wasn't. My legs didn't want to push up when I opened the car door. My hands shook and my heart was the judge's gavel, constantly being pounded against that little round piece of wood. I only wished it would create order inside my body the way that gavel forced order in a court.

My feet were like bricks as I walked up a side alley where houses were lined with bushes out front. A stud with long dreads stood on the steps, blowing out cigarette smoke.

"What up, young? You lost?"

"Yeah, I'm looking for 2865."

"Turn left, right around that gate." She pointed. "It's should be the third gate to your left."

"Thanks."

"No problem," she said and watched me until I turned.

Just like she said, it was the third gate to my left. I pushed it and entered a tiny yard with no grass. A small barbeque grill sat in a corner and a little table that was more for a patio took up seventy-five percent of the space.

I walked up to the door and held my fist up, still pondering if I should knock. I could've made up a lie and told Tasia that she didn't want to see me.

But I wasn't a coward and I wouldn't start being one right then. I tapped on the door softly at first, then my knocks got bold. I stepped back when I heard shuffling.

"I'm coming!" a woman yelled.

I heard two locks and the door eased open. I almost fainted and so did the exact replica of myself when she looked me in my eyes. I didn't even have to tell her who I was. Tears drained from her eyes and she damn near fell on me, squeezing me so tightly that I couldn't breathe.

"Thank you, Jesus. Thank you, Jesus," she chanted. Her tears soaked my collar and before I realized it, my own were clouding my vision. She stood rocking me from side to side, and for a moment, I thought we would stay there forever, just sniffing and blubbering. I knew, in that instant, that she didn't just hand me over to the state willy nilly.

She released me and wiped her eyes. "I'm so sorry. Please forgive me. I'm sure you didn't want a stranger hugging all on you like that. Come in. Only if you like."

I followed her into her little townhouse. It was neat. A tall wooden cabinet with glass doors set against a wall and it was filled with crosses and decorated plates. A wooden table sat in front of that with four chairs and place mats.

She had a television against the wall and a sofa in the corner just big enough for a nap and some soap opera watching.

"Have a seat. Are you thirsty? Hungry?"

"I'm okay," I said, drying my own tears.

We must have sat there for twenty whole minutes not saying a word. Neither of us knew how to approach the other.

"Well, I know you have questions."

"Only one."

"What is it?"

"Why? Why you'd give me up?"

Her lip got to quivering and she couldn't look me in the eyes.

"I was fourteen when I got pregnant with you. Your father was seventeen. Both of us were foolish. We thought we'd run away and figure out how to feed you later."

"Why would you run?"

"Kevin was white and I was black. There was no way in hell they'd let us live in peace in a place like McComb, Mississippi,"

"So, I *was* born there."

She nodded.

"How long was I there for?"

"Until you were seven months. It was a waiting game. Kevin made a deal with his father that if you didn't get any darker than the color you were born, we'd get to keep you. I agreed to see what would happen, but something in me knew better."

"What about your parents?"

"They weren't having it. They said having a baby with a white man put all of us in danger. After you were born, I gave you to Kevin and his parents and after seven months, you were gone." Her tears started to reform. "I begged them to tell me where you were and they slammed the door in my face."

"Who named me?"

"Kevin."

A tear fell from my eye. They both wanted me. They loved me.

"I wish I could tell you more, but I don't know anything else. Kevin's father left the state with you in tow and it was the last we saw of you. Last year, when some lady from Kansas contacted me, I almost didn't believe her. But here you are." She smiled.

I couldn't control my emotions. I let my face fall into my hands and the tears—that seemed to come more frequently these days—flowed and

215

flooded. I would never know the whole story of how I got lost in the system, but at least I knew they wanted me.

"Where is my father?" I asked, choking on my tears.

She wiped her tears away and a faint smile reared. She reached for my hands and I braced myself for bad news but instead she turned her head toward the stairs. "Kevin!" she yelled. A tall man with my eyes and jawline like mine lugged himself down the stairs. He wore a plaid shirt and faded light blue jeans. He stopped midway, looked at Minnie, then at me, back at Minnie, and then back at me again. His knees betrayed him and he used the wall to catch himself.

Both of my parents were right there. *Right there.*

"Do you know who that is?" she asked.

He didn't have much breath to speak with. "That's… that's my baby girl."

He ran to me and they both held onto me for dear life. Unlike my mother, my father was not timid. He held on to me like he'd known me for years. He kissed my face and admired my features.

"How did you find us?" he asked.

"I didn't. My foster mother did."

"God bless her," he said and grabbed my hand to hold it. "Sit down next to me." Tears still ran down his face, but he didn't care. "My God you're beautiful."

"Are you hungry or anthing? Did you travel a long way?" My mother asked.

"I'm okay. I came from Atlanta."

"All alone?" she asked.

"No, my girl…" I hesiated, "…friend is outside in the car."

"You left her outside? Go get her. Let us meet her."

I smiled and wiped my eyes. My father stood when I stood, still holding my hand. I smiled at him and he walked with me to retrieve Tasia. He refused to let me out of his sight.

Tasia joined us inside and fell into the crying fest as my parents told me more of their story.

"Your father and I lived in two different neighborhoods. My daddy worked for his in a lumber yard. I was only twelve when I first met him. He was fifteen and he did some work at his daddy's yard, too, on the weekends." She still smiled when she talked about him, like he wasn't even in the room. "He was always nice to me. Bought me sodas and candy from the vending machines with his labor money and told me silly race jokes about white people. It was funnier coming from a white boy. It wasn't until I was fifteen that he made a move on me, obviously." She laughed."By then I had grown up a bit and deveopled in grown-up places."

Tasia reached for my hand and smiled as she listended and squeezed my fingers.

"I was walking home from school and his daddy had gotten him a new pick-up for his seventeenth birthday. Kevin offered me a ride home when he passed me walking up the road. Me and my daddy had had a fight earlier that morning. I don't remember about what, but I didn't want to go home. Kevin took me to a park and we sat in his truck listening to music, going back and forth between his music taste and mine. We both liked a little bit of the others genre. The more we talked, the more we realized we had a lot in common, even though we were different skin tones. Kevin, you can jump in whenever you're ready."

"You're telling the story just fine." He smiled.

Both of them still had southern accents and it made me laugh.

"Well, fine. Anyways, Kevin wasn't shy about what he wanted. He asked me if I thought he would be too old for me and I told him no since my daddy was ten years older than my mama. He thought I wouldn't be able to handle a mature relationship and what mature people did until I kissed him first to shut him up."

"Had you kissed anyone before him, Mrs. Coursey?" Tasia asked.

"Yes, this boy name Melvin. It was gross." She laughed.

"Yeah, because it wasn't me," Kevin boasted.

"Whatever." She swatted his shoulder. "Kevin was the last boy I kissed."

"How did you two get to stay together?" I asked, now ready to skip the gushy details and get down to the nitty-gritty.

Kevin decided to answer that question. "Well, after my daddy took you away and didn't return with you, he and I fought every day. I needed to find a way to make a living, so he couldn't run my life anymore. I went down to the recruiting office and joined the military as soon as I made eighteen. Your mama cried her eyes out, but it was the only way. The military kept me away for a year. And the year after that, her daddy kept us apart. Once Minnie made eighteen, I took her away in the middle of the night. We drove until we couldn't anymore. We had to get out of the south. I had a little money, so I got us a place in Kentucky, but we didn't too much like it there either. We drove all the way here and made ourselves a living and a home."

"Do you talk to your parents?" I asked Minnie.

"My mother visits and my daddy passed away,"she said.

"My parents shut me out the day I joined the military," said Kevin.

"You don't regret it?" I asked.

Kevin shook his head no. "Looking at you, it was the best decision I ever made."

There were the tears again.

"I'm so happy you found us," Minnie cried. "Shoot, all this crying done made me hungry. Let's go out and celebrate. My baby's home!"

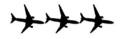

We sat down to eat at Copper Canyon Grill. I pulled out twenty singles and handed them to Tasia for her to stack neatly in the middle of the table. My parents looked at one another with confused faces.

"You don't have to tip until after the meal." Kevin said.

I laughed. "It's something Tasia does when we go out."

"It's something *we* do when we go out." Tasia looked into my eyes and smiled. She was right. I'd started pulling out the money without thinking. I'd created a routine with somebody. Maybe I'd figure out my favorite food too.

Tasia explained our system to my parents and I watched her realizing that she and I could have what they had. Money wasn't everything. After what my parents went through, they endured. I wanted to endure my tribulations too. I had a love and she was everything despite my shortcomings.

I hear you, Kitty. I hear you.

Epilogue

Junction City, Kansas

"Mama! Tasia and I are heading out."

"Be careful. You know planes fall out of the sky."

"Nothing is one-hundred percent safe."

"And tell your daddy to bring me back something to cook. I need to get some seasoning imported or something. The south wasn't the best place to live, but at least the food tasted like something."

Tasia and I laughed.

I'd moved my mother and father into the house I owned in Kansas after giving Barry the money for taking care of it and paying the taxes on it that I didn't know existed. I didn't even ask why he did it. I was learning a lot when it came to responsibility. I'd even gotten myself a bank account.

Tasia and I both enrolled in school. She was taking up education after learning that my mother was a teacher. She felt inspired. I majored in criminal justice and hopefully I'd get into a law school when the time came.

Tasia and I talked about becoming foster parents when we were stable. We both wanted to help kids like us. For now, she had a part-time job at the grocery store and while she was at work, I spent time with my parents.

I learned that my father talked in his sleep just like me, and he loved music. I was shocked to learn that I got my love for dance from him as well. My mother wasn't into any of that. She loved books and that was where we found common ground.

"You girls ready to go?" my dad asked with his hand up on the popped trunk.

"We'll be back tomorrow, Dad. We don't have that much luggage. Close the trunk."

"Oh, I didn't know." He shrugged then walked around to the driver's side. The wind was blowing unnecessarily hard that day. A little dry heat might have been just what I needed.

My dad dropped us off at the airport and we waved goodbye. We went in to retrieve the tickets we booked online and the clerk did a double take when I approached the counter.

"Your name is Siren, right?"

"No."

"Wait, no, I heard you go by Cream now. I watch you on YouTube all the time. Do you still dance?"

"Only for birthday parties and that's also the only time that I go by Cream. My name is Kelli."

She smiled and handed us our tickets. "Have a safe trip Ms. Kelli." She nodded and I nodded back, pulling Tasia by the hand.

We hurried to our terminal since we were running a few minutes behind. I was nervous about this trip, but not as nervous as I was when I met my parents. I didn't want to be late.

We boarded our plane and, like usual, I fell asleep instantly. In a few hours, I woke up in Dallas and we hurried to grab our rental.

It was a long ride to Hutchins State Prison, but it was one I was willing to take. Tasia and I both rode with our sun glasses on and the windows down.

We pulled up and there he was. Corey walked with a bag over his shoulder. I stepped out of the car and removed my shades. He smiled and dropped his bag. He ran over to me and hugged me like he knew me all my life, the same way my daddy did. Tasia stepped out of the car too, smiling.

"You must be Tasia," he said.

She nodded.

"Damn," he said. "That is scary. You look just like my sister."

"She must have been beautiful."

"You've never seen a picture?" He raised his brow.

She shook her head no.

Corey looked to me.

"I didn't want to freak her out." I laughed.

He wrapped his arm around my shoulder. "Thank you for coming. Thank you for everything. Kitty was lucky."

"No, I was lucky. Let's get you out of here, before they change their minds about this release," I teased.

We all got into the car and as Tasia went to turn the ignition, I grabbed her hand to stop her.

"What?"

"I think I'll drive."

Stud Life Series

www.christiana-harrell.com

CPSIA information can be obtained at www.ICGtesting.com
Printed in the USA
BVOW05s1718160215

387946BV00013B/240/P